T0194472

GUNNING FOR HOSTAGES!

The sun hadn't been up half an hour when the Carstons boldly rode into David Workman's camp. . . . "Kind of early, ain't it lawman?" said Workman. . . .

"You'd better produce the two women and be quick about it," Chance said. "You've got about one minute before I start taking you and your camp apart piece by piece."

David Workman gave out a loud guffaw, a crude sort of laugh, Chance thought. It was a defiant noise too.

"Best listen to him, Workman," Handy's loud voice said off to the side of the camp.

By now Workman's crew was up and armed, ready for a fight if their boss called for it. "Sullivan!" Workman called out and one of his men stood up, hauling Ella Mae and Rachel Ferris to their feet. But rather than use the women for a shield, he was foolish enough to stand one on each side of him.

Handy Partree brought his rifle up to his shoulder, took dead aim on the man's chest, and fired once. . . .

Books by Jim Miller

The Stranger from Nowhere
Carston's Law
Shootout in Sendero
Stagecoach to Fort Dodge
The 600 Mile Stretch
Rangers Reunited
Too Many Drifters
Hell with the Hide Off
The Long Rope
Rangers' Revenge

Published by Pocket Books

10

THE EX-RANGERS

THE STRANGER FROM NOWHERE

JIM MILLER

POCKET BOOKS

New York   London   Toronto   Sydney   Tokyo   Singapore

This book is a work of fiction. Names, characters, places and incidents are either products of the author's imagination or are used fictitiously. Any resemblance to actual events or locales or persons, living or dead, is entirely coincidental.

An *Original* Publication of POCKET BOOKS

POCKET BOOKS, a division of Simon & Schuster Inc
1230 Avenue of the Americas, New York, NY 10020.

ISBN: 978-1-5011-0993-5

First Pocket Books printing June 1993

10 9 8 7 6 5 4 3 2 1

POCKET and colophon are registered trademarks of Simon & Schuster Inc.

Cover art by Garin Baker

Printed in the U.S.A.

For John McCabe,
who knows the true meaning of friendship.

CHAPTER
★ 1 ★

Handy Partree was a giant of a man. More than six feet tall, his muscular frame held over two hundred pounds, not an ounce of which was fat. The only person who had ever been able to put him in his place had been his mother, a strong-willed woman if ever there was one. Not that plenty of men hadn't tried. And Ron Gentry was finding out how hard that was right now.

A man of medium build, Gentry swung out at Handy Partree, hitting him square on the jaw with a hard right roundhouse punch. But aside from the feeling that he had struck a solid rock with his fist, sending shock waves up his arm, the only expression on his face was one of surprise at the look of the big man before him. As hard as he had hit him, the blow didn't appear to faze Handy at all. Rather, if seemed to infuriate him. It was that outraged look that Gentry immediately regretted.

With a big hamlike fist, Handy grabbed Gentry by the throat and proceeded to slap him back and forth, knocking his head about as though he were toying with a rag doll and not a man. The crowd that had gathered began to laugh at the silliness of it all. Like all crowds, it had gathered for the entertainment of the event.

"All right, what's going on here?" a man wearing a badge said as he made his way through the crowd. Seeing the viselike grip the big man had on Gentry, he said, "Let him go, Handy, you're killing him." Having spent most of his life taking orders from white men, Handy Partree did just that, and the crowd watched an unconscious Ron Gentry fall to the ground. "Break it up, folks, the fun's over with for now," the city marshal of Panhandle added, kneeling down beside Gentry to see how badly the man was hurt.

"He ass for it," Handy said humbly. His mama had always told him to mind his manners, a piece of advice he had taken to heart many years ago. "I din' start it. Honest."

The whole affair had taken place at the entrance to the livery stable, where Handy had been taking care of a chore he had been handed that morning. The livery man, who had seen it all, stepped forward now.

"He's right, Abe. Ron Gentry was acting his usual piss-ugly mean self," he said. "And you know Gentry, he ain't no lover of coloreds to begin with. Cussed him something fierce, then hit Handy twice before he got laid out. That's the truth of it."

"That right?" Abe Forrest asked Handy, the beginning of a scowl on his face. This was 1868, and you couldn't give a black man orders the way you could once upon a time. Had to treat them nice. Equality, some were calling it. Abe Forrest didn't particularly like it, but the law was the law. Besides, Handy Partree was a pretty nice man for a colored, once you got to know him.

"Das a fact, suh." Handy nodded yes in an adamant gesture.

"Maybe you'd better finish up your business here and get back to Morrison's spread," the marshal suggested.

"Jes' finished ma las' hoss," Handy said, and went about his business as though nothing had happened. He didn't even rub the part of his jaw that Gentry had hit so hard. But then, this wasn't the first fight Handy Partree had ever been in.

Ever since the end of the war and the beginning of what they were calling Reconstruction, many a black man had headed for parts unknown to make a new life for himself, but Handy Partree wasn't one of them. Oh, he'd left the man who had owned him as a slave, but he had only wandered down the road a few miles to take up employment on Henry Morrison's ranch. He hadn't gotten the name Handy for nothing, working as a blacksmith and doing a little bit of everything else around the Morrison spread, whatever Mr. Morrison wanted or needed done. He'd even taken a liking to Morrison, an odd feeling considering the man was white. But Morrison was fair, and to Handy, you couldn't ask for more than that. And Handy was making a living wage besides.

Henry Morrison, Handy had found out over the past three years, had served in the Union army as a captain in a cavalry unit of sorts. Although he never did brag about the war and his exploits, like some, Handy got the distinct impression that the man was likely some kind of hero in that troubled time. When the war was over, Morrison had gone back to a small ranch he'd run before the war, up here in the northernmost part of Texas, taking Handy Partree on as one of the first half-dozen men he hired. Every one of them was a veteran of the war, had fought for the Confederacy, and managed to get along well with both Morrison and Handy. At first it had been a real challenge.

"I hear there was trouble in town," Morrison said to Handy when he had returned to his employer's spread. The boss had found him in the bunkhouse, looking into a small hand mirror and testing his jawbone, which was just now starting to feel the effects of Ron Gentry's blows. Morrison was only a little above average in height, but still managed to talk tough, as though he were speaking to one of his cavalry troopers in the war. His no-nonsense tone had gotten Handy's respect right off.

"Making it trouble 'pends on who side you on, I reckon," Handy said, looking Morrison square in the eye. "I been ordered about and beat all mah life, so it weren't nothing new to me."

But Morrison insisted Handy tell about it, so he did. Handy told his boss everything, including how Gentry, who was working on getting drunk, had spit in his face and called him a no good nigger. When the name-calling didn't goad Handy into a fight, Gentry had proceeded to push him about and finally slapped him hard across the face.

"Sorry, boss, but dat was too much," Handy said almost apologetically. Then, with a fierceness in his eyes, and a challenge in his voice, he said to Morrison, "No white man haff to take dat, do he, boss? Do he?"

"No, Handy. I don't blame you one bit," Morrison

said agreeably. "Listen, don't you worry about what other *white* men don't have to take. You just remember what I say *my* men don't have to take. You didn't do nothing wrong." When he found Handy had little else to say, he turned to leave, then stopped at the door of the bunkhouse and faced the big man. "For what it's worth, if it was me Gentry tried that stuff with, I'd have killed him on the spot."

Then Morrison was gone and Handy knew for a fact that his boss would indeed have killed Ron Gentry right then and there.

Two days later Handy accompanied Morrison into Panhandle. Their purpose was to get supplies, which the cook was complaining about again, but that wasn't how things turned out that day. Handy had just finished loading the supplies in the wagon around noon, when the general store's owner's son came charging in, all excited about something.

"There's gonna be fireworks for sure!" he yelled, spewing spit all over the counter.

"Slow down, son, just slow down," the boy's father said.

"Can't!" Then the boy turned his gaze to Handy. "Your boss is in for it, Handy. Called Ron Gentry outta the saloon, says he wants to give him a thrashing!"

"Billy, go get the marshal," the store owner said, suddenly in a hurry himself. "Abe Forrest is likely over sweet-talking that millinery woman. Now, go!"

Handy rushed to the entrance to the general store, looked down the street and saw Gentry push several people out of his way as he made his way toward Henry Morrison, who stood right in the middle of the main street for all to see. Handy was making his own way toward the buckboard when the store owner brushed past him, as excited as the rest at what was about to take place. After all, everyone liked a good fight, especially when they weren't in it.

Out on the main street, a bravado-filled Ron Gentry stopped about fifteen feet from Henry Morrison, who seemed bent on beating the living tar out of the town bully, if the look on his face was any indication.

"Ain't falling for it, Morrison," Gentry said with a shake of his head. "I've seen you in a fight or two. You're too good with your fists. But with guns, well, I'm a mite better at that. Care to give it a try?" He seemed to be downright cocky, even pushy about his prowess with a six-gun, and for a second it shook Morrison.

"I'm no gunman, Gentry, and you know it," Morrison said, playing Gentry's game of words and throwing them right back at him.

Ron Gentry shrugged, a sneer on his face. "Don't have to be a gunman, just good with a gun." He undid the leather thong holding his revolver in place. "I think we'll try our fighting with guns instead of fists today." The sneer widened into a look on the man that was pure confidence.

Henry Morrison still carried his old Colt's Army Model .44 in the standard-issue cavalry holster, planted on his right hip with the pistol butt forward. He didn't want to fight this man with a six-gun, but there didn't seem to be much choice, so he undid the flap on his holster, all the time wondering how he could outmaneuver this man. Then he remembered back to his days during the war, to an incident he'd been a part of with one of his sergeants.

"I don't know about you, Gentry, but I'm all of a sudden getting awful hot," Morrison said. If he sounded nervous, it was because he was, not sure in his own mind whether this hastily formed plan would work. This was a different time, a different man he was facing, a different place. With one movement of his arm, he ran his sleeve across his brow, which was indeed filling with sweat. Then, as he slowly pulled his hand away, he grabbed the brim of his hat, as though to take it off.

He was doing this when Gentry, full of overconfidence, snarled, "Nervous, Morrison?" By the time he had his words out, Morrison had set his hat a-sail, with the results that he wanted. While tossing the hat at Ron Gentry as a distraction, Morrison had yanked out his Colt's revolver.

The hat diverted Gentry, but only for a second, as his hand went down for the gun at his side. By the time Morrison had his Colt's out and was aiming it at Gentry, his opponent had already fired once, hitting Morrison in the chest, knocking him back and making a small pool of blood form on the man's shirt front.

Morrison snapped a shot off at Gentry as he reeled backward, almost certain his mark was true. He saw Gentry fall back, but there was something strange about him. As he lay there on the street, he could have sworn he'd fired only one shot. Or was he seeing double now?

Ron Gentry lay dead in the street, and Henry Morrison was surely dying by the time Handy had rushed to his boss's side. In fact, Morrison knew he was dying.

"He's dead, boss," Handy said, his eyes filling with tears at the sight of Morrison laying there, all bloody and dying. "You got him good."

"You tell Epp the place is his now," Morrison said, spitting blood out with his words. "He's a good man."

"I'll do that, boss."

7

Morrison squinted at Handy then, giving him a stare as though he were a stranger he didn't know. But then he did know. He knew it all. The bullet holes, all of it! With his last strength, he grabbed Handy's arm and squeezed it in desperation.

"You best move on, Handy," he said, blood still coming out of his mouth as he spoke. "A friend of mine, one of my sergeants, lives down south of here. Twin Rifles. Chance Carston. You see him. He's a good man too."

Then he died.

Handy Partree picked up Morrison's body, stopping only to look down at the lifeless body of Ron Gentry and spit on it before placing Morrison in the buckboard and taking him home.

He told Epp what had happened and what the dying Morrison had said, about him taking over the spread and all. Then he buried Henry Morrison, in an area the man had often talked about setting aside for his future wife and children if he ever had them. Before the day was out, Handy Partree had collected the hundred dollars that he had coming to him and left the Morrison spread, the dying words of his boss on his mind.

He never looked back.

CHAPTER

★ **2** ★

If anyone noticed Handy Partree when he rode into Twin Rifles, it was more because he was a stranger than the fact that he was big and black as the bottom of a well-used coffeepot. Although it was a small town in the southern part of Texas, the citizenry of Twin Rifles had seen their fair share of strangers ride through. Some had been Mexican in extraction, some claimed to be peaceful Indians—although it was hard telling these days just how you could describe a peaceful Indian since most of them carried weapons of one type or another—but for the most part the majority of the drifters who had come through this border town had been white men who had fought in the War Between the States. And most of them had yet to find a job or a place they wanted to settle down near.

What made the citizens of Twin Rifles so suspicious of the drifters passing through their town, no matter what the color of their skin might be, was the fact that twice in the past few years some of those drifters had tried to empty the town's bank of its money without making the proper withdrawal request. The population deeply frowned on such illegal actions. But Handy Partree just figured the suspicious looks were little more than the normal hatred for his race, which he'd encountered in the South during his lifetime. Not that a man ever got used to it. It was just something that was . . . well, it was there.

It was late in the morning when he rode into town. He could have stopped at any one of the stores in town to ask for the information he needed, but decided he'd give a try at the local saloon first. After all, they'd been telling him he was free for several years now. Still, he did feel strange when he tied his horse to the hitching rail in front of Ernie Johnson's Saloon that day.

He felt stranger yet when he stepped inside the establishment and squinted at the men inhabiting the place this early in the day. Not that there were that many customers. The place wasn't even half full, but those who were here seemed to be enjoying their drinks. Once his eyes were adjusted to the dimness of the saloon, he thought he spotted the man he was looking for and made his way over to the bar, taking a place beside him.

"Eff you got somethin' cold ta drink, I'd like a glass of it, please," Handy said in his most polite tone of voice. He pulled a dollar coin from his pocket, knowing full well he would have to show he could pay for what he was ordering, and likely pay first. Handy had found out during those few recent years of freedom that some things didn't change. For example, five times out of eight the man behind the bar would figure him for a shiftless nigger, no matter how hard he worked.

"I don't know," the bartender said as he surveyed the room to see if any customers were leaving. It was still a time when, free man or not, some white southerners wouldn't drink in the same room with a black man. Since the bartender was also the proprietor, Ernie Johnson, he was making sure his profits weren't going to be cut into by this man's presence.

"Go ahead and serve him, Ernie," the man next to Handy said good-naturedly. He even offered Handy a brief smile.

"Thankee, suh," Handy said, smiling himself as he nodded to the man.

"Don't mention it."

Handy had picked the man because he wore an old cavalry hat, its front brim pushed up and pinned back by what most likely were the crossed saber emblems the man had worn during the war. And Henry Morrison, in his dying words, had spoken of one of "his sergeants." Morrison being a cavalry officer, Handy naturally figured this was the man he had spoken of.

"How's water?" Ernie Johnson said, placing a glass of what looked like fairly clear water before Handy. "It's about as close as I can get to chilled liquid around here." More than likely, Ernie Johnson had ducked out the back door, grabbed hold of some boy lazing about, and sent him down to the local creek to fetch a glass of water.

Handy smiled in appreciation. "Believe me, mista, long as it ain' no more brackish than the stuff I bin drinkin' fo' the las' week, I'll drink it."

"I could get you some goat milk—" Ernie started to say.

11

But Handy interrupted the man, holding a large hand up, showing the flat of it to the bartender. "Please, I ain' *dat* bad off." With that he took his own sweet time drinking the glass of water. When he set the empty glass down before him, he noticed that his dollar was still there.

"Water's free, even to *your* kind," he heard a stranger say to him, but it wasn't the man with the cavalry hat. When Handy turned to look at him, he saw that the man was as gruff in feature as his voice sounded, and it was a raspy one to be sure. It only took one whiff to realize that the man was also pretty drunk.

Ignoring the drunk, Handy turned to the man on his left, the one he intended to speak to about Henry Morrison and his days during the war when they were both in the cavalry. But he didn't seem destined to have that conversation.

"Hey, nigger, I'm talking to you!" the man all but screamed at him, grabbing his arm to shift Handy's position.

"Look, mista—" was all Handy got out before the drunk took a swing at him. Drunk as he was, the man still hit him hard in the mouth, knocking his head sideward.

It was a mistake.

Before the man knew it, Handy had grabbed him by the throat, nearly wrapping his big fist about the man's entire neck. The drunk immediately regretted it, if the angry look in Handy's eyes was any indication.

Ernie Johnson had seen his place torn up too many times to let it happen again. By the time Handy had his hand around the drunk's throat, Ernie had a

12

sawed-off shotgun in his hands and was making sure everyone saw that he had it.

"Mister," he said to Handy, "I don't care how big you are, I know for a fact you ain't got the kind of money to pay for damages to what you're gonna bust up. So take it outside."

Handy nodded silently and proceeded to march forward to the bat-wing doors. With the drunk facing him, his actions made the man walk backward, stumbling half the time. When Handy had paraded his opponent out onto the boardwalk, he stepped back, let go of the man's throat, and hit him hard enough to make him sleep off his drunk clear into next Tuesday. The man spun around in a circle twice and fell off the boardwalk onto the ground next to Handy's horse, unconscious.

"What the hell!" was what he heard next from his rear. But before he could turn, someone had grabbed him from behind and was trying to spin him around, likely to take a poke at him. Ducking, he felt a whoosh above him as he half spun and stuck his hand out in a fist. He hit his mark, someone's underbelly. As quickly as he stood straight up, hoping to hit the someone with his head, that somebody was gone.

He had to look about to see what was going on before he caught sight of the man with the cavalry hat slamming the man who apparently swung at him up against the wall of the saloon. Then, by grabbing the man, who seemed to be as big as the first one who had come at him inside, Mr. Cavalry Hat pulled him off the wall, half turned him about, and hit him hard enough to send him sprawling down in the dust, as unconscious as the first man.

"I'm obliged, mista," Handy said, now standing

beside Mr. Cavalry Hat. Looking down on the two men, he added, "Neva did take to being called a nigga."

"Don't blame you, friend," Mr. Cavalry Hat said. "No man likes being name-called."

"I'm Handy—"

"I'll say." Mr. Cavalry Hat looked down at the men on the street and shook his head in what might have been admiration. "That's Carny and Wilson Hadley laying there, you know. Meaner than skunks and smell twicet as bad when they been drinking. And they been drinking."

"Am I suppose to be impressed?" Handy asked.

"Son, let's put it this way," Mr. Cavalry Hat said with cocked eyebrow. "If their brothers was here too, we'd likely still be fighting instead of having this conversation."

"I see, Mista Carston."

"Huh?"

"You look like a Chance Carston I'm lookin' fo'," Handy said. "With the cavalry hat I thought you was—"

"Oh, no. Emmett. That's my name." Emmett stuck out a hand to Handy, apparently not afraid to see if the color would rub off on him like some white folks were. "Nice to meet you."

"Me too. Ma name's Handy. Handy Partree."

And they shook hands.

"Where you come from, Handy?" Emmett asked in a cordial manner.

Handy gave a half smile and shrugged. "Nowhere."

"Well, where you going?"

The noncommittal shrug again. "Same place."

"I see." The tone of Emmett's voice was enough to

14

convey the fact that he had decided to mind his own business. At least for now.

Emmett's gaze traveled halfway down the block as his arm shot out before him. "Now, Handy, if you're looking for Chance Carston, why, that would be him right over there."

Handy's stare followed Emmett's as he took in the figure of a big man leaving the marshal's office.

And he wasn't wearing a cavalry hat.

CHAPTER

★ 3 ★

There was one thing about being a westerner that differed quite a bit from the lifestyles east of the Mississippi. That difference, and it was a big one to a black man at the end of the War Between the States, was that people west of the Mississippi knew that there were two things you couldn't blame a man for being. The first was his heritage and the second was his name. No man had a hell of a lot to say about who his ancestors were or what his name would be, for he didn't have anything to say about it to begin with. Such decisions had already been made for him. When Handy Partree first met Chance Carston, he got the impression that the man held firm to that line of thought.

"Chance here was a cavalryman in the war, just like me," Emmett said once he'd introduced Handy to the big Texan. Chance himself was over six feet tall, lacking three or four inches that Handy had on him. He had smiled and acted just as friendly as Emmett when introduced to Handy. "Old Chance, he taken to one of them newfangled John B's when he come back from the war. Me, I always did like this bent-up old thing," Emmett added with what was meant to be a shy smile as he doffed his turned up cavalry hat and held it out at a distance, as though to admire it the way a painter does his painting.

"Well, Mr. Partree, you look like you've been on the trail a while," Chance said when Emmett got through admiring his cavalry hat. "Why don't you two join me over at the Ferris House for a meal." To Handy he added, "Best food in town."

"Sounds fine to me," was Handy's reply. "I gotta tell you, that saloon serves a troublesome glass of water, cold or not."

"I'll pass this time, Chance," Emmett said, digging out his pocket watch and seeing that it was approaching the noon hour. "If I don't get back to the ranch, Greta will shoot me for holding up the meal." It was hard telling whether Emmett was leaving because his wife had indeed prepared a noon meal for him, or if it was simply that he knew Chance and Handy had some private business to transact. Either way, he was soon mounting his steed and heading out of town to his ranch, which was not far from Twin Rifles.

The Ferris House was the only boardinghouse in Twin Rifles. It was run by Margaret Ferris and her daughter Rachel, a beautiful young woman who took after her mother. She had also taken a liking to Chance, and he had returned the compliment with a kiss or two of his own when no one else was near them.

"I figured you'd be making your way over here about now," Rachel said with a smile when Chance and Handy entered the boardinghouse and immediately headed for the community table the Ferris women managed to keep filled with customers on a regular basis.

At first Chance stopped at the near side of the long table, about to take a seat next to three or four customers about to finish their meals, then thought better of it and moved on down to the far end of the community table, where he and Handy took a seat by themselves.

"More privacy," he said by way of explanation to the big man, although in the back of his mind he knew Handy Partree was likely suspicioning he had done it to keep from starting any trouble with the folks now seated and taking in their meals. When Rachel had taken their orders, Chance leaned across the table and, in a lower voice, said, "Now then, you mentioned something about Henry Morrison telling you to come see me. Care to tell me just what it is he had in mind?" he added with a sly smile. "I ain't seen old Hard Ass since the end of the war. How's he doing these days?"

A sad look came over Handy as he looked at Chance and said, "I'm 'fraid he's dead, suh."

Chance couldn't believe what he was hearing, and the look about him said just that. "Where? When? Henry and me went through too much for either one of us to die easy," he said, mad at the death of his longtime friend. But then, soldiers are like that, thinking themselves invincible once they have beaten the odds on the battlefield.

Handy told him how Henry Morrison had died, most of it, anyway. There were some aspects he left out at the moment, facets of the whole thing he didn't believe needed to be told right now. Maybe later. Maybe.

Once he was through talking, Chance had a frown on his forehead that said he still wasn't clear about what had taken place, and why Handy had sought him out. "That still doesn't explain why Henry would want you to come and see me," he said, cutting loose a piece of meat loaf Rachel had served them both about halfway through Handy's story.

But Handy was quick to offer up a logical reason. "Near as I can figger, the boss was thinkin' Ron Gentry's friends would be taking out after me," he said with an informal shrug. "Gentry, he worked for Mr. Workman."

"And who is this Workman?" Chance asked around a mouthful of food. Even the death of a friend hadn't dulled the man's appetite. "Why would he come after you?"

There was a wrinkle in Handy's brow as he said, "David Workman, he used to *own* me 'fore the war was over." It seemed obvious that the big man didn't like that one particular word, and with good reason. "He's a hateful man who don' like being proved wrong." Before Chance could reply, Handy set down his fork and opened the top buttons on his shirt, pulling open one side of it enough for Chance to see the thick scars produced from the whippings he'd received.

"Real hateful, I'd say," Chance said after getting a good look at Handy's chest. Pushing his empty plate aside, Chance was silent for a moment as he took a sip of coffee. "You figure this Workman will try tracking you down?"

"Wouldn't surprise me, no suh."

"You know much about breaking horses, Handy?" Chance asked, cocking a curious eye at the man across the table from him.

"Not really. Why do you ask?"

"Man's got to make a living. I reckon I'm offering you a job," Chance said with a bit of a crooked smile.

"Pardon me, Mr. Carston—"

"Chance."

"All right, Chance. But why is it you offering me a job?" Handy asked, apparently mystified by the proposition.

Rachel appeared out of nowhere and began clearing off the table, within easy earshot of what the two men were discussing.

"I reckon it's like this, Handy," Chance explained. "More than one man out here has been hired to work for an outfit, even though he was wanted by the law three counties over. This Workman fella comes looking for you, let him look. You're working for me."

Rachel stopped what she was doing and broke out in laughter.

"And what's so funny?" Chance asked, taken aback by her actions.

"Don't you let him fool you, mister," she said with a mischievous grin.

"Oh?" Now she had Handy interested.

"Chance is just figuring that whoever it is that's coming after you is gonna give him a reason to start a fight," Rachel said, still grinning as though she knew it all. "And if there's one thing Chance Carston loves to do, it's *fight!*"

Chance sloshed on his hat and handed the black man his own John B. Although he would never admit it, Rachel had spoken the truth, and at the moment it put him in an embarrassing situation.

"Pay no attention to that woman. She's daft," Chance said, guiding Handy by the elbow toward the front door. "Let's get our horses and I'll show you around the spread."

Rachel was still laughing as they left.

CHAPTER

★ 4 ★

I don't know, Handy," Chance said as he watched the black man land on his backside again, the wild mustang he'd been perched upon running off to the far side of the corral. As big as the man was, the horse had had no trouble throwing him. Still, Chance thought, he had to give the man credit for trying. Most men would have quit a couple of days into busting that bronc, which had turned out to be one of the meanest Chance could recall trying to break. But Handy had about as much bottom as that mustang he'd been trying to ride. He had been out at the Carston ranch for the better part of a week now, trying to learn the not-so-gentle art of breaking a wild mustang. "I'm beginning to believe you were right when you said you didn't know spit about breaking horses."

Handy shrugged, beating his hat against the side of his pants as he limped toward his new boss, seated on the top rung of the corral. It was hard for Chance to tell whether the man was trying to beat the dust from his hat or his denims, both appeared so full of it.

"Take a break and get you some water, and we'll have a go at it again shortly," Chance said, then jumped down from the corral.

"Where's your brother?" Handy asked, scooping up a handful of water from a nearby trough. "Don't he do no riding?"

"Over to the barn," was Chance's reply with a nod. "I told Wash he could start shoeing a couple of that last string we busted. They're ready for it."

George Washington Carston, better known as G.W., or Wash, had returned from picking up a few more wild mustangs the day before. At first he was a bit more than surprised to see Handy on their spread. A veteran of the War Between the States, he had fought on the side of the Confederacy, and didn't quite feel easy about the decision his brother had made to take on Handy Partree. But Sarah Ann, his wife, had calmed him down and assured him that Handy had been a first-class gentleman the entire week. As for the duty of shoeing the horses, it was Wash who had made the decision that he would rather work alone doing that than be forced to work with this stranger. Chance was just making it sound as though he was the one who made all the major decisions around here, which wasn't the entire truth.

Handy had a desperate desire to sit down for a while, but the only seat he spotted was a bench over by the barn, where Wash was hammering away at a horseshoe.

"Mind eff I sit?" he asked Wash, more out of politeness than anything else, once he had ambled over toward the bench.

"Go ahead," the younger Carston brother said in a cold, stiff manner. If he was giving the impression that he meant to ignore this man, he was doing a good job of it, for he didn't even look up at Handy. "It's a free country, ain't it?"

"So I hear." Handy took a seat and watched Wash as he went about trying to fashion a horseshoe to its proper size. It only took a minute to see that the man was no blacksmith.

Handy was soon on his feet, his hat propped back on his head, his hand wrapped around Wash's hammer in midair as Wash once again attempted to pound the iron piece. "Here, let me show you how it's done," Handy said without being pushy.

"You sure you want to do that?" Wash said, glaring back at him as he released his grip.

"What horse it goin' on?"

Wash indicated the horse he was about to shoe, and Handy glanced at the shoe, then at the horse. He lifted up the rear foot of the now tame mustang, eyed it, and returned to the fire and the horseshoe. In what looked like an effortless manner, he soon had the red-hot horseshoe over the anvil and was pounding it to the shape that would fit the horse's left rear foot.

"I may not be able to break one of you horses, but I can shoe 'em better'n you can," Handy said to Chance when he came over to the anvil. Chance appeared to be as impressed as his brother was over the man's ability to properly form a horseshoe.

"I reckon a man's got to be good at something," Chance conceded. "And you definitely ain't no great shakes as a bronco buster."

24

"How 'bout you and you brother break them horses and I shoe 'em for you?" Handy said, sticking the horseshoe into a bucket of water to cool it.

"That kind of work will last only as long as we got horses to break," Chance said.

"Yeah. What would you do in the time in between shoeings?" Wash said with a frown. Apparently, Wash thought Chance was still wary of the man. Maybe wondering if Handy Partree wasn't nothing more than a shiftless nigger?

Handy scratched his jawline briefly and said, "Seems ta me Miss Sarah Ann said somethin' this mornin' 'bout you brotha bein' too damn lazy to chop a proper portion of wood for the stove." By the time the words were out, a hint of a smile had come to his face as he looked at Wash. "I can take care of dat betwixt times."

"All right," Wash said, sticking out his hand to the man. "You've got a deal." More than once, Wash had wound up chopping wood for Sarah Ann's stove when Chance was involved with trying to break a mustang and claimed he didn't have time to do it. Of course, Chance was never short on taking second helpings once the meal was put on the table either. So having the extra help around to pick up some of the slack would be a relief to all of them, even he had to admit.

"Agreed," Handy replied, and took Wash's hand in the good faith with which it was given.

The three of them worked well that way, Chance and Wash breaking the horses, and Handy Partree shoeing them when they were broken enough to ride.

It took both Chance and Wash another day and a half to break the hell-raiser Handy had last been thrown from. But they did it, and in late morning of the second day Handy had been shoeing horses,

25

Chance told everyone to take it easy, they would finish their work in the afternoon.

"Saddle our horses, Wash, and I'll buy the three of us a meal at the Ferris House," he said, wiping a fair amount of sweat from his brow. The sun had risen higher and hotter that day than it had in quite some time, and the work had seemed harder and much slower than in days gone by.

"I'll take my meal over at the Porter Cafe," Wash replied as he turned to get the horses.

"Then you'll pay for your own grub, brother." Chance knew good and well that Sarah Ann, Wash's wife, still worked at the Porter Cafe as a waitress, which always gave him an easy out for not buying his brother a meal. At times Chance could be as cheap as a Mexican whore.

When they entered Twin Rifles, Wash headed for the Porter Cafe, and Chance and Handy pulled up in front of the Ferris House. Chance thought he saw movement behind one of the curtains on the second story, wondering who in the world could be making beds at a time like this. When mealtime arrived, it was usually a sure bet that both Margaret and Rachel Ferris could be found serving up meals at the community table, one of them working the kitchen while the other took orders and poured coffee. As quickly as it occurred to him, Chance dismissed the thought of who it might be he'd seen up there. When it came to mealtime, he tended to concentrate on the food placed before him—or what he was fixing to eat beforehand.

They took the same seats they had when Handy had previously eaten there, right at the very end of the community table, the end nearest the kitchen area. It was then Chance noticed Handy squinting toward the kitchen entrance, especially when Rachel was walking in or out of it.

"See something special back there?" Chance asked.

"Could be." Then, to Rachel as she passed by him, Handy added, "Begging you pardon, ma'am, but who dat be setting inside you kitchen?"

Rachel stared at the man in disbelief at first, not sure what he was talking about. Then, when Margaret entered the eating area with a platter of food, she thought she saw what had attracted the man's attention. "Oh, you mean Ella Mae. I don't blame you," she said with a smile. Momentarily, she disappeared into the kitchen area, back with Ella Mae in tow. "Handy, I'd like you to meet Ella Mae. We just hired her the other day to help out with the bed-making and cleaning up around here."

As soon as Rachel had started to introduce the young black woman, Handy was struggling in an awkward way to get to his feet, like a gentleman was supposed to do when being properly introduced to a lady.

"How do, ma'am," Handy said, knowing that he must be feeling as out of sorts as this woman before him. Ella Mae quietly took his hand, smiled at Handy, then made a comment to Rachel about getting back to eat her meal. Then she was gone. But not before Handy could take in her features.

He at once thought that Ella Mae was the most beautiful woman he had ever seen. She was short and otherwise average in build, but had the prettiest smile he'd ever come across. Her hair had been braided, and her eyes seemed so alive when she smiled at him that Handy couldn't help but wonder how she could have taken a job like this. Still, she was in a maid's uniform, the pert black and white standard dress of all the maids he had ever seen. Watching her go, he wondered if he would ever see her—or have cause to see her—again.

"Stand there like that much longer, Handy, and your eyes are likely to drop out," Chance said with a grin. "They sure are big enough to set loose from your sockets."

"Oh, sorry." Chance knew how gawky Handy must have thought he looked, and felt. Handy plunked down on his hardwood seat, still gazing at the now closed kitchen door.

"I've seen that look before, you know." It was a strange, raspy voice. But it was enough to divert Chance's attention from the empty doorway. When he turned toward the voice, he saw a grizzled old-timer, dressed in buckskins and wearing the oldest beaver hat he'd ever seen.

Dallas Bodeen was now as much a resident of Twin Rifles as the Carston family, and he was a friend to all. In fact, other than being an outspoken old mountain man who had once ridden with Will, Chance, and Wash Carston as a Texas Ranger, he was still an active man for his age. Not that he knew his age. As far back as Dallas could remember, he had kept track of time in years by the battles and fights he'd been in. There was the Mexican War, and the Battle of Pierre's Hole with those Gros Ventres back in '32, and of course those fracases in Texas. But then, there was always a fracas in Texas somewhere. A body was either fighting the Mexes or the Comanches.

"Don't let him get to you, Handy." Chance smiled and introduced the two men, pointing out Handy's newfound job as a blacksmith on the ranch. Dallas was simply identified as a local troublemaker.

Rachel took the orders of all three men, and Chance

explained to Dallas how good a job Handy was doing
for him. "Trouble is, when I git through here pretty
soon, there ain't gonna be enough work to keep him
around permanent," he added when Rachel brought
them plates of roast beef, pan-fried potatoes, and
biscuits.

All three knew the value of a hot meal on the
frontier. A man didn't waste any time eating it lest it
become cold as the very devil himself, and cold food
was far from satisfying to anyone's palate. They ate in
silence, the most noise any of them made coming
from the rattle of their coffee cups to the saucers they
sat on. It didn't take but fifteen minutes to finish the
meal, and it was Dallas who broke the silence.

"Say, Handy, I been thinking," he said in a pensive
tone. He took a sip of his coffee, nearly burning his
mouth before realizing that Rachel had just refilled all
of their cups with the scalding liquid. "Old Harvey
Reed, he runs the livery here in town. I was a-talking
to him just the other day, and he was telling me he's
had hisself a whole pile of work he's had to turn away
'cause he cain't handle the livery and that forge of his,
both. Smithy work, you understand?"

"I see." Chance could see from the surprised look
on Handy's face that he found it hard to believe as
many white men in this town had tried to help him
along as had in the past week or so.

"You could come down to the livery now, ary you
like, and I'll introduce you to Harvey," Dallas said.
"Nice as any man Mama ever told you the world was
full of."

"What do you think, Chance?" Handy asked, looking to his boss.

"Oh, don't worry 'bout him, Handy," the old
mountain man scoffed. "Chance ain't gonna do noth-

ing but sit here and try to sweet-talk Miss Rachel for the next half hour, anyway."

"I reckon we got little enough work to spare an extra half hour, Handy," Chance said as he smiled. "See you then."

As he watched Dallas and Handy leave, Chance thought he had seen a look on Handy's face that reminded him of the way he'd felt when he'd returned in one piece after the war was over and saw Rachel that first time. Now it was three years later, and look what had happened to the two of them. He found himself looking seductively at Rachel as these thoughts passed through his mind.

"Chance, you wipe that leer off your face or I'll do it for you," Rachel said in an authoritative voice.

"If it'll get you any closer to me, give it a try," Chance said, and the grin on his face widened.

CHAPTER
★ 5 ★

Harvey Reed turned out to be as pleasant and easy-going as Dallas Bodeen had said. In fact, he was more than pleased that a man with the talents of Handy Partree would agree to do some smithy work for him in a week or so, which was just a little longer than Handy figured it would take to shoe the rest of the mustangs that Chance and his brother were breaking.

"Shore does beat all," Handy said with a bit of disbelief as he and Dallas walked back to the Ferris House.

"What's that?"

"Other than them Hadley Brothers—or whatever they name is—I got treated mighty well by the folks in this town," he said. "Man of my skin color, he don' see dat too often."

31

"Well, I reckon you've hit on it 'bout right, brother," Dallas said as they continued their stroll down the boardwalk. "Folks hereabouts is mighty nice. Even a crusty old piece of leather like me gets treated with a fair amount of respect, and you won't find that too awful much in any town that ain't within sight of the Stony Mountains."

"You have much to do with the coloreds in your trade?" Handy asked out of curiosity.

"Oh, shore, we had our share of Negroes or whatever you wanted to call 'em," Dallas nodded. "Beckwourth was the best known, I reckon. Jim Beckwourth. Mulatto, he was. Took to liking the Crows and become one of their chiefs, believe it or not. And of course there was Edward Rose, but he was more of a bad apple than anything else. Never was real sure 'bout him. A real scamp, that one was.

"Go back way before my time, why, they say there was a fella named Esteban or Estebanito, whichever. Man of your color. Trekked along down in Old Mexico back in the fourteen hundreds, I do believe it was. Him and Cabez deBaca. Got theyselves kilt, just like everyone else in this land does eventually."

"You know quite a bit about this country," Handy commented, "or at least the parts of it that you inhabited."

"Rocky Mountain College is where I learned it all." Dallas smiled proudly, knowing full well that there was no such school by that name in this territory and state. But it always sounded impressive to those he told it to. What had happened was, during those long winter months that he and Will Carston had been trappers, well, they had whiled away their spare time by doing all there really was to do, which was read. Each man would bring along two or three books and they would exchange volumes with one another during the winter months. Some men broadened their knowledge by such reading, while others learned how to read this way. With Dallas Bodeen it was a bit of both. He had read some of Shakespeare, as well as *Clarke's Commentaries on the Bible,* some of James Fenimore Cooper's works, and even some nature and science books that were floating around camp. But he had learned to read well, and yes, he had learned a lot he'd never known about the world and this country's history, as little as it might seem at the time.

"Sorry to say, mah friend, but you don't look like any school-learned man I ever saw." There was a hint of a smile on Handy's face as he spoke now. "Not who wore buckskins, anyway."

Dallas smiled at the man beside him. "Let's just say I'm a self-made man."

"Well, they's one thing 'bout a sef-made man," Handy said, smiling back.

"Oh? And what's that?"

Handy's smile grew wider as he said, "Can't blame nobody but you for what you do."

Dallas stopped in front of the Ferris House, where Chance was waiting for them, engaged in small talk with Rachel. Rubbing his chin in thought, Dallas said, "Yeah, I reckon you're right, Handy."

When Chance and Handy had mounted up and were ready to leave, Dallas said, "I'd keep an eye on this one, Chance. He's got more twixt his ears than muscle." As he watched the two ride out of town, Dallas turned to Rachel and added, "That he has. Yes, sir."

It only took four more days to shoe the horses that Chance and Wash finished breaking, and it was at the end of that fourth day that Chance approached Handy. But first Chance had to wait for Sarah Ann to finish with him.

Handy Partree had always taken his meals at the Carston house away from the Carston family. Even in the chill of the early morning, he would take his plate of food and find a place to sit outside the house, on the front porch or the back stoop, or maybe that bench he had discovered that first day he'd gone from being a bronco buster to a blacksmith. He was sitting on the porch, finishing the last of his meal and the last of his coffee, when Sarah Ann came out with her coffeepot in hand.

"I'll take that," she said, and took his empty plate as she refilled his cup.

"Thankee, ma'am."

"Is there something about my food you don't like?" she asked him outright. You didn't live around a man like Big John Porter, her father, and learn how to be anything but direct with people, even when you tried.

"Oh no, ma'am," Handy said, suddenly looking as though he had offended the woman, and desperate not to. "No, ma'am, you fix a fine plate."

"Then why is it you always find someplace other than my kitchen table to eat?" she asked, trying her hardest to sound tactful. "And you never ask for seconds, not like Chance or even Wash."

"I don't sit at you table, ma'am, 'cause I ain't got you husband's approval," he said humbly. "Believe me, I can tell when I ain't wanted 'round."

"Why, that's nonsense!" she said in a wide-eyed manner. "I'll straighten that out right away. You listen to me, Handy Partree. That table of mine has got four sides to it, and by the way I figure it, that's just enough to fit the four of us when I cook a meal. Tomorrow

34

morning you take a seat at my kitchen table or I'll *really* be perturbed!"

"Yes, ma'am," he replied dutifully, knowing better than to argue with a woman with a temper.

Then she was gone, disappearing back into the house in total silence. But it was a silence that spoke volumes.

"She can be a tough one, all right," Chance said with a grin as he approached Handy, his own half-filled coffee cup in hand.

"So I see."

Chance took a seat beside Handy, and the two silently drank coffee in what was left of the evening light. When he had nearly finished his, Chance casually tossed the remnants into the dust and set the cup down beside him.

"Listen, we got the horses and the shoeing pretty much taken care of today."

Handy nodded agreement.

"And you've got a couple of days before you're going to work over to Harvey Reed's, right?"

Again Handy nodded.

"Well, Wash and me are gonna trail that herd over to the Fort Griffin area tomorrow. Thought maybe you'd like to come along with us," Chance said, trying to sound as casual as possible. "It'll give you an idea of what some of the land over that way looks like, in case you've never been there, you know."

Handy shrugged. "Whatever you say, boss."

The next morning, Handy was about to take his plate from the kitchen table when he remembered the stern lecturing he'd gotten from Sarah Ann the night before. So he took a seat at the place set for him, where Chance was already seated and eating as though there were no tomorrow. Handy was cutting a piece of ham when Wash entered the room and, as he took his seat, gave him the most god-awful scowl Handy thought the man could conjure up.

"Morning," he said to Chance and Sarah Ann, obviously ignoring Handy. Sarah Ann returned his greeting, doing her best to be as pert and jovial as she could. Chance would have choked on his own words had he tried to speak, as much food as he was shoveling down his gullet.

Sarah Ann was about to have a seat now that the men were all served, when she saw Wash give his best downright-mean scowl to Handy. Suddenly her eyes got moist as she kicked Wash under the table.

"Ouch!"

"How could you embarrass me this way!" she said just before tears silently began to roll down her cheeks.

Wash, upset, began to rise from the table, but was abruptly plunked down in his place as Handy put a big hand on his shoulder. "No. You stay, I'll go. It's you house anyway," he said, knowing he was the cause of the trouble between these two young people. Then he picked up his plate and coffee cup and headed for the front porch. By the time he'd taken a seat and begun to eat again, he could hear the raised voices of Sarah Ann and Wash inside.

"Good thing I finished right quick," Chance said as he too left the house, appearing at Handy's side on the porch. "God help us if they start throwing the silverware," he added with a half smile.

Handy soon finished his meal, having no more taste for it, although he knew he would need the nourishment before the day was out. He set down his plate and coffee cup and got up, doing a half turn to head back into the house when Chance caught hold of his arm.

"Believe me, Handy, you don't want to go back in there," he said, once he had the man's attention.

"But they still arguing, likely ovuh me."

"They tell me it's all part of love," Chance said, "which is why I'm still a bachelor."

"Ain't you gonna stop 'em?" Handy said in a worried tone.

"I'd rather fight the five Hadley Brothers—all at once and alone!—than come between those two right now," Chance said, dead serious.

"You shore?"

"Handy, they'll fight like cats and dogs until the day they die, and still outlive you and me both." Chance looked back at the house and slowly shook his head. "First thing I found out after they got married was how full of energy they are. If you get my drift."

Handy nodded. "I think so."

"Come on, let's get the horses. Maybe they'll calm down by then."

Handy gave a quick glance back at the house as he and Chance walked toward the barn. "Yeah. That sound like a good idea."

It was.

CHAPTER
★ 6 ★

The sun was just making itself known to the world when they left that morning, herding all of a dozen mustangs Chance and Wash had broken over the last couple of months. Two men could have done the job with ease. Hell, one man could likely have done the job without an awful lot of trouble. So three of them were really unnecessary on this trip. Which might leave one to wonder why in the devil there were three of them herding all of a dozen mustangs anyway.

But to Chance there was a method behind this madness, which indeed it was if you thought about it. Oh, he could have brought along Handy Partree and done the job with just the two of them. That would have been easy enough. That would leave Wash at home, still so much in love with his wife, Sarah Ann, and still missing her as much as he did when they had to leave home. Hell, almost as much as she missed him. But damn it, the two of them would have to learn how to live apart once in a while during this marriage. Why, look at that cattle drive they had made with Charlie Goodnight. Wash hadn't been worth a damn the first half of that drive, all because he was lovesick over Sarah Ann. Pure foolishness, it was!

No, sir, Chance Carston never was one for doing things the easy way. For the most part he got along fine with his brother now, even if the two of them had served on opposite sides in that damned War Between the States, which had been over a good three years. And Chance got along right fine with Handy, although he hadn't known him all that long. The problem on this spread was the divisiveness that apparently was taking place between Handy and Chance's brother. Chance knew he could have suggested that Wash and Handy take the herd of mustangs over to Fort Griffin by their lonesome, but he knew good and well that the two of them would likely kill one another over some damn thing, and then where would he be? Why, the mustangs would go off loose and he'd wind up breaking horses all by himself and taking care of a widow woman who wasn't all that fond of him in the first place—neither one being a prospect he cherished doing. Not by a long shot.

No, Chance wasn't about to do things the easy way. He had recognized the problem between his brother and Handy right off, and he'd done some mulling over on it from the start. By the time they had finished breaking and shoeing those mustangs, Chance had come up with the idea of all three of them taking the horses up north to Lieutenant Callahan at Fort Griffin. And somewhere along the way he figured he would straighten these two compadres of his out. He wasn't sure how he'd do it yet, but somehow they had to be straightened out. Hell, a man couldn't run an outfit with a couple of peckerwoods like Wash and Handy feeling like they did toward one another. Why, a body would never get a lick of work done!

Chance also knew that his brother didn't have to say a word when they left that morning. Why, you could see in his eyes that he was glad Handy was coming along. Likely had some crazy-ass notion in his mind that Handy would go off and rape his wife if he got the chance, while the Carston brothers were away. And Chance knew good and well that if he could see it, why, Handy Partree had likely caught on to it long before him.

So when they took the herd out that morning, you could say it was a mite frostier than usual, and the weather had nothing whatsoever to do with it.

"Remember when we took that herd of horses up this trail back in sixty-six, Wash?" he asked his brother when they took a short break about mid-morning, letting the horses drink their fill at a nearby water hole.

"How could I *not* forget it?" Wash scowled, his bad mood still very much a part of him. Normally, he enjoyed these trips when the two of them would be off selling their horses to the army, the prospect of bringing back a few hundred dollars in the front of their minds and thoughts. "You keep shoving it down my throat every time I turn around."

It was back in 1866 that the two of them had agreed to break and have ready for Charlie Goodnight upward of sixty horses in the early spring. The two of them had spent the better part of the springtime breaking those mustangs, then herding them up to Goodnight at old Fort Belknap. That also turned out to be the place Goodnight had gathered a couple thousand head of longhorn cattle and struck out across the Llano Estacado, the Staked Plains area, and on into New Mexico with them. The Carston brothers had been foolish enough to join him in his adventure, and had made a good deal of money along the way. But it was an experience that Wash, for reasons of his own, would choose to forget if he could, and Chance knew it. Being his older brother, he just wasn't going to let Wash forget it.

"Had more blisters on my ass that spring than I ever did the whole four years I rode for the cavalry in the war," Chance said to Handy with a smile.

Handy nodded noncommittally. "Sounds like."

They had stopped for several minutes, to refresh themselves, and Wash seemed to be ignoring them both, apparently caught up in his own line of thought.

"Where did you serve in the war?" Handy asked Wash after several minutes of silence. Chance wasn't sure whether it was a mistake or not. Not until his brother answered Handy. The war, after all, had never been one of the great conversation pieces between the two brothers, and he wasn't sure what all his brother had done during that conflict. Not that he really cared. All that seemed important since the war had ended was the fact that they had both made it back alive and in one piece.

"Believe me, mister, you don't want to know," was Wash's hard reply as he mounted his horse and swung about to gather up the mustangs and move them on their way.

Chance could do little more than shrug hopelessly at Handy when Partree gave him a confused look. Silently the two mounted their own horses and lit out after the younger Carston, who was now driving the small herd of mustangs hard into the north, toward Fort Griffin.

When the sun had reached high noon, Wash was still pushing the mustangs as hard as he could without putting them in any more danger than they already were. But the whole time, Chance found himself wondering that it must be some sort of miracle that his brother hadn't run one of those steeds into a gopher hole someplace, causing the lot of them to trample one another and break a few legs. It simply didn't make an awful lot of sense, as hard as Wash was driving them. The trouble was, neither Chance nor Handy could for the life of them figure out what it was that had happened to Wash to make him act this way.

By late afternoon Wash had run the herd a good thirty some miles. Of that Chance was sure. They had passed up a couple of the normal water holes they made stops at, the horses being pushed on their way by Wash, who was now acting something close to a madman, Chance thought. It was when they stopped at that last water hole that Chance rode up to his brother, reining in his horse and as ready for a fight between them as he had ever been.

"We'll make camp here tonight," he growled, just waiting for some smart-aleck remark from Wash.

"Sure," was Wash's reply, a touch of madness about his face as he half smiled back at his brother. "Whatever you say."

But Chance was almost itching for a fight now, and getting pushy. "Git that wild hair outta your system, little brother?"

"Not really. Just toned it down a mite. For now." Then Wash jerked his reins to the side and was gone, galloping off to the other side of the water hole, apparently to be alone in his thoughts.

42

Chance gathered up some firewood, and Handy set about putting on some coffee and some of the meat they had brought along for an evening meal.

"Didn't mean to set you off like dat," Handy said in an apologetic way when Wash entered camp and quietly took a seat at the fire.

"Some days are worse than others." Once again all Chance could do was give Handy a perplexing shrug when the big man glanced his way for a possible explanation of his brother's remarks.

They ate in relative silence, although none of the three had a taste for the food that night. Whatever it was that was bothering Wash had some sort of strange effect on Chance and Handy, if for no other reason than the three had to work together for the next few days. And no man wanted to work with someone who had a wild hair up his keister, especially when neither of the other two was sure what in the devil it was that had started the whole thing.

"You know, brother, you've always been a mite on the shy side," Chance said when he'd finished his meal and poured them all an extra cup of coffee. "But you've been quieter than that ever since you come back from the war. Something happen to you during the war, did it?"

Wash had finished drinking half of his cup of coffee. After Chance had spoken, the younger Carston looked at him, slowly shook his head in disbelief, looked down at the remains of the cup and tossed them to the ground in disgust.

"One thing I gotta say about you, Chance, you don't know when to shut up," he said in a voice that was now sad and mad at the same time, if that were possible. "You just can't let it go, can you?"

"Look, I—"

"No, Chance, I didn't have a lot of heroic things happen to me during the war, not like you and Emmett sit around talking about." Wash frowned. To his side, Handy was taking the whole thing in, not sure whether he should speak or not. "No, most of what happened to me was pretty goddamn tragic. That's what war really is, Chance. That's what it really is, *brother.*"

"Well, forget I ever—"

"No, you wanted to know, so you might as well find out." Then he turned to Handy, a somewhat wicked look on his face. "You want to know what unit I was in?"

Handy shrugged, suddenly feeling as though the whole thing was his fault, all for asking one lousy question. "Don't haff to."

"I was with Terry's Texas Rangers."

"So?" No reaction.

Wash was concentrating on Handy now, all but ignoring his brother's presence. He fed it to him one piece of bait at a time, knowing that when he said the right words, Handy's facial expression would change to one nearly as gruesome as the way he was feeling.

"How about General Nathan Bedford Forrest? I served under him."

Handy raised an eyebrow in partial recognition. Chance simply sat to the side, stunned by what was taking place before him.

"How about the Battle of Fort Pillow? You recognize that?"

Handy's face grew suddenly dark, a vicious hatred coming to him now. He most definitely recognized that name, that battle.

Wash nodded, satisfied he had gotten his point across.

"What the hell's going on?" Chance finally said. "What the hell are you talking about, Wash?"

"Oh, I forgot, Chance, you wouldn't have heard of this place. You and Emmett was never in a losing battle, was you?" Without waiting for a reply, he added, "It was a Union defeat, Chance. And more than just a few Union soldiers died that day."

"Yeah." From the look of him, Handy could reach out and choke Wash with those big hands of his at any moment, he was that filled with hate. "A lot mo'n jes' white Yankees. Lots mo'." If Handy hadn't been there, he damn sure knew of it.

"What the hell is the Battle of Fort Pillow?" Chance asked, still puzzled about what was disturbing his brother.

"It was probably the worst goddamn day I had to live in that war," Wash replied, his voice almost dead of tone.

He looked off at the ball of fire that was the setting sun, and he could see it all like it was yesterday. Only yesterday.

It had all started for Wash Carston on April 12, 1864, one year before the war ended. The men of Terry's Texas Rangers were then a part of Major General Nathan Bedford Forrest's Confederate Cavalry Corps, and Wash Carston was among them. It was at six A.M. when Wash and his unit took part in the assault of Fort Pillow.

A Tennessee earthwork fortification, located on the Mississippi River bank, it was forty miles north of Memphis. The garrison held the Union's Thirteenth Tennessee Cavalry, 295 men strong, and the Eleventh U.S. Colored Troops, with 262 black men. The Confederates had fifteen hundred men, outnumbering the Union soldiers by a three-to-one margin.

The Confederate forces took a good part of the garrison that morning, and there was talk of Union forces surrendering. Twice the Confederates, now under General Nathan Bedford Forrest, demanded the Union surrender, but with little results, even after flags of truce were raised. It was late in the afternoon when the Confederates got resupplied with ammunition and the tragedy of the day took place.

The Confederates charged the last line of works, driving the Federal troops to a nearby bluff, down the riverbank and directly into the face of the Confederate soldiers of one Captain Anderson, who had maneuvered his men there earlier. That was when it all began. Or did it? No one has ever really known for certain.

The Confederates only lost a hundred men that day, with fourteen men killed and eighty-six wounded. They captured 226 Federals, wounded one hundred, and killed 231. Of the 262 men of the Eleventh U.S. Colored Troops, only fifty-eight were taken prisoner. Many of the rest of those black men were killed that day, and it was those black men, those black faces, that Wash Carston would never forget.

"Some of the Federals we took prisoner claimed that when we scaled the earthworks we were screaming slurs at the black troops as they threw down their arms and surrendered. They claimed we were killing unarmed men," Wash said softly, reliving the day in his mind as he looked out to the horizon. "Others claimed we were killing wounded soldiers, black and white, where they lay that day.

"I heard others of our men, our Johnny Rebs, who said some of those blacks was picking up their rifles to fight after they claimed to have surrendered, and that was why they killed 'em.

"For what it's worth," Wash added, turning his attention to Handy now, who seemed totally wrapped up in the younger Carston's tale, "some of the men I was with that day said those colored soldiers were the last ones to break and run. I reckon that says something for the kind of courage they could muster."

Wash paused a moment to catch his breath, but neither Chance nor Handy interrupted the man, knowing he was reliving a moment he would likely just as soon forget but knew he never could.

"I don't know if they'll ever know the truth of what happened that day. All I know is I didn't shoot anyone who wasn't running at me with a rifle in his hand or trying to bayonet me." He said this last to Handy in particular, as though it bore some importance. "I never shot a man in the back, and I never shot an unarmed man, no matter what his color," Wash said. "And that's the truth."

"I believe you," Chance said in an earnest tone.

"You jes' figgered once I found out where you'd been, I'd hate your guts, so you beat me to it and set out to hate me first, that it?" Handy said, now quite calm.

"Something like that."

Handy scratched the side of his head, as though in thought, before saying, "Mama say they's good in all men. Jes' dat sometime you gotta look for it. You ask dat woman of yours what she see in you. She din' find no good, she be long gone."

"Well, what do you know." Chance smiled. "A smithy and a philosopher both."

Handy grinned. "Shoot, Chance, I was to worry 'bout mah slavin' days, I be dead from fretting a long time back." Handy said in what he must have visioned an emphatic tone.

"You got a point," Chance said.

"Slavin' days is ovuh for me."

Chance looked at his brother, who now had a mournful look about him. "And the war's over, Wash."

"I die soon nuff without I hurry it 'long." At this last, Handy smiled, to himself as well as anyone else who might see him.

Wash nodded slowly to himself as he rolled out his bedroll. The man just might have something there.

CHAPTER
★ 7 ★

By the time they broke camp the next morning, Chance had come to the conclusion that his brother and Handy might get along after all. Chance had awakened to Handy stirring about camp, building a fire and measuring out coffee for the pot. It was before light, the sun still a grayish dusting of orange on the eastern horizon. But there was movement about on the plains and in the small grove of cottonwoods they had made camp near, so he knew it wouldn't be long before the rest of the world was awake.

What had surprised him that morning was the fact that Wash, who was the last one to rise, had actually mumbled a morning greeting to the black man, who smiled back at him in a genial way. It was then Chance thought he had done a good job of straightening the two out.

Just after daylight they broke camp and began to move the horses north again toward Fort Griffin. But this time they were on a far more open stretch of prairie, and all three of them had a hand in urging the small herd of mustangs on. By the time the sun was hot and overhead, they stopped for a dry camp near another water hole. Handy had noticed that the distance between water holes was getting farther and farther.

"Musta come a good twenty miles this mornin'," he said over a cup of water and one of Sarah Ann's biscuits, which made up the noon meal for all three of them.

"Close to it, I'd say," Wash agreed with a nod.

"Could be more, maybe twenty-five," Chance said around a mouthful of biscuit. "It was a far piece, I know that."

"Just what's up around this Fort Griffin you headed for dat wants hosses?" Handy asked when he'd finished his water.

"The army," Chance said. "Found out after we come back from the war that they're still needing good mounts for their men. Just like when the two of us was in it."

"That doesn't seem to ever change," Wash said. Both he and his brother had found out early on in the war that being in the cavalry required a good steed under you at all times, and the cavalry units of both the North and the South were in constant need of good horses.

"We run across a young lieutenant named Callahan who was in need of good mustangs for his men. He was also the purchasing agent for his post," Chance said. "Claimed he could always use more good mounts, so whenever Wash and me get a bunch of 'em broke, why, we head up this way with 'em and sell 'em to the army at twenty-five dollars a head."

"Sounds like fair money for the work I seen you put into taming dese brutes," Handy commented in an offhand manner.

"We like to think so." Wash continued to sound a whole lot more pleasant toward the Carstons' new hired hand than the day before, Chance noticed. Hopefully, it would stay that way.

"It wasn't until last year that Lieutenant Callahan and his men got transferred to Fort Griffin when it opened," Chance said. "Used to be he was stationed at a little outpost not far from us at Twin Rifles. Now it's a good seventy miles we have to travel to get to Callahan."

"Drive these mustangs like we did this morning, and we should be able to make the fort by late this afternoon, don't you think?" Wash asked his brother.

"Seems about right," the older Carston said, nodding in concurrence.

They filled their canteens with fresh water and got the mustangs moving again, each of them confident they could make Fort Griffin by day's end. There were maybe two more water holes and a lot of flat ground between them and the military post, so there was no reason they couldn't finish this job by suppertime.

The afternoon was hot, but they pushed the mustangs to their limit, stopping only to water them once about mid-afternoon. While the herd drank its fill, the three of them loosened the cinches of their own mounts and let them blow before drinking. All three had enough experience with the four-legged animals to know that a good riding horse must be cared for properly, especially when it's ridden hard.

They were within an hour of sundown when Fort

Griffin came in sight. Established during the summer of 1867, the fort held four companies of the Sixth Cavalry. It was first named Fort Wilson, but the post was soon renamed in honor of Major General Charles Griffin, who commanded the Department of Texas. Aside from officers' and enlisted men's quarters, the fort itself contained an adjutant's office, a hospital, guardhouse, magazine, five storehouses, forage houses, a bakery, four stable sheds, and workshops. The mission of the men of this garrison varied, including duties such as escorting the government mail, surveying parties and cattle drives, and punishing depredating Indians in the territory.

"Got a guard on your corral tonight?" Chance asked the guard at the gate when they arrived.

"Every night, sir," was the young man's answer.

"Good. I've got a dozen new mustangs for your cavalrymen. Now, where can I find Lieutenant Callahan?" Chance said.

The young private indicated the officers' mess tent, and Chance told Wash and Handy to stay with the herd while he hunted up the lieutenant. Callahan was just leaving the mess tent when Chance found him. Their greeting was anything but businesslike, the lieutenant offering a hearty handshake and a slap on the arm to Chance as though he were a long-lost brother.

"It's good to see you again, Chance," the officer, a lieutenant in his mid-twenties, said cordially. "What have you got for me this time?"

"How does a dozen mustangs suit you?"

"Just fine." Chance could tell by the lieutenant's voice that the man was glad to have anything he and his brother could get to him. Chance also knew that as long as it was in reasonably good health, had four legs, and could be ridden by a cavalryman of the United States Army, Lieutenant Callahan didn't really care what the animal was. "I'll take a look at them tomorrow morning and draw up a voucher for you. Why don't you and your brother get some food over at the officers' mess. It's not bad tonight."

"Can I bring a friend?" Chance asked. "He helped us with the herd this time."

"By all means," Callahan said with a smile. "After you're through eating, why don't you come over to the new sutler's store we have. You can usually get a decent drink there after duty hours." The young officer took in Chance's dusty figure and gave a mischievous smile. "And I can see that it's definitely after duty hours for you."

Chance returned the smile. "Ain't that the truth."

Callahan then took Chance, Wash, and Handy over to the post stables, where he had the stable hand rub down and feed their mounts for them. Chance noticed that there was a bit of hesitancy in Callahan when he first introduced him to Handy outside the post gate. He was sure that both Wash and Handy noticed it too.

Callahan left them then, for he had other duties to perform before meeting the Carstons at the sutler's store. He said he had sent word to the officers' mess to have food ready for them when they arrived.

They were greeted at the mess tent by a gruff-looking man in an apron, apparently the cook or one of his assistants. At first he seemed polite enough, telling them to enter the tent and have a seat; the food and drink were already set on a table. Then he saw Handy enter, and turned back.

"Sorry gents," he said, "but I'm closing the mess tent down for the night." The trouble was, now he was acting as though he had to work real hard to sound civil. Or maybe it was because he had a less than welcome tone in his voice and spent the better part of his time staring at Handy in a none too friendly way.

"Why, you—" Chance started to say, pushing himself away from the table, knowing full well what this man was about. And being typical of Chance and his way of approaching things, he was about to meet the man head on with his fists. But Handy, seated to his left, placed a big hand on his shoulder and slowly shook his head as Chance turned his glare toward him.

"Don' make no neva mind, boss," Handy said in an even tone, he too now rising from his seat. "Spent mosta mah life eatin' out back." Then, picking up his plate, utensils, and coffee cup, he silently left the mess tent. Chance gave the cook a hard look, then, frowning, silently followed Handy's example, ending up outside. Wash did the same.

Outside, the three squatted down Indian fashion, just like they always did before a campfire, and ate in silence. But this time there wasn't any campfire.

"That wasn't right, what he did in there," Wash finally said, placing his plate down on the ground beside him. Chance was careful to take in his brother's face as he spoke, certain in the dimming evening light that Wash wasn't speaking simply to be patronizing. Neither he nor Wash had been brought up to be that way. Pa had made sure of that.

"No, it weren't," Handy said sadly.

"But you're *free!*" Wash added, emphasizing the last word.

"Ah may be free, but dat don' mean day gotta *like* me," the black man mumbled, almost beneath his breath.

"I don't think any man's ever really free as long as

he has to put up with the kind of bull men like that shove at him," Chance said, tossing a thumb over his shoulder at the mess tent. When no one responded to his words, he added, "Let's go get us a drink. The lieutenant said he'd buy us one."

The sutler's store still had the smell of freshly cut wood about it, along with the aroma that brand new goods seem to add to a store when it first opens. The newness of it all was an invitation to enter the building, even from the boardwalk outside, Chance noticed. There were only a handful of men in the store when they entered, but they were soon gone. Chance was sure that were it not for the insistence of the lieutenant, the owner of the store would have refused to serve them altogether. The real reason, underlying it all, was of course the fact that they had Handy Partree with them.

"No thanks," he said when the lieutenant offered him a shot glass of whiskey. "I'll jes' look around."

"Listen, boy, you keep your hands off the merchandise," said the owner, a harsh-looking man with what appeared to be a permanent frown on his forehead.

"Don't worry about him, mister," Chance said, a frown crossing his own face. "I trusted him with more than a thousand dollars worth of horseflesh on the way here and never lost a wink of sleep the whole time."

"That's a fact, friend," Wash added. "I was there, and we got here with everything we started out with. If he says he's looking, then he's looking and that's that."

But no matter what Chance and Wash said, the owner still had a distrusting aversion to Handy, and every once in a while Chance saw the man sneak a look out of the corner of his eye at their compadre, likely wanting to catch him tucking away something of value in his shirt. What Chance couldn't understand was how the man could possibly keep track of where anybody was in his store, considering how dimly lit the place was in the evening hour.

The Carstons and Callahan spent upward of half an hour sharing a couple of drinks and reminiscing over what had happened since the last time they had seen one another. Chance had only taken two drinks during the whole time and was feeling more than a bit relaxed when a bearded man entered the store and made his way to the counter. He wasn't particularly big so much as he was thick across the chest. "Make way for a real man," he growled as he sidled up to Chance and elbowed him out of the way. Quickly joined by two others, he was apparently used to having his way.

"Easy, mister, there's plenty of room," Chance said, trying to be friendly even if the new customer wasn't. But he didn't like the pushy manners of this one, not one bit at all.

"You tell him, Mr. Workman," the bearded man's friend said with a leer.

Workman must have liked that kind of support from his friends, or whoever these peckerwoods with him were, for he took another step closer to Chance and once again tried to nudge his side with an elbow. He was plain looking for a fight, this one.

Chance moved his own arm over the area he expected the man to hit him, then half turned and grabbed his elbow, spinning the man around to face him. This time any friendliness about the bearded man was gone. "I said take it easy, mister," he said in a growl that was just as mean as this Workman character wanted to make himself.

"Look, fellas, I don't want no fighting in here," the owner of the sutler's store said, a twinge of nervousness in his voice now. "This place is brand new, you know, and I don't want it busted up or nothing."

Without taking his eyes off Workman, Chance said, "Believe me, I ain't looking for a fight. I've put in a rough day and all I want is a peaceful drink before I call it a night."

"Don't worry, Barney," the lieutenant said with a friendly smile, addressing the store owner, "Chance won't hit him. Will you, Chance?"

"No, I won't hit him." The older Carston's eyes were still trained on Workman, suspicious of what the man might do next.

But Workman seemed to want to push it for as much as he could, and grabbed a fistful of Chance's faded blue work shirt. "A real mama's boy, huh? Lieutenant's got you under his thumb," he snarled, trying to throw in a degrading laugh with his words.

"Mister, if that was a new shirt, I'd kill you where you stand," Chance hissed in his own mean tone. "But it's the only shirt I've got, so you can count yourself lucky."

Lieutenant Callahan saw the hate growing in Chance's eyes, heard the same thing in his voice, and was determined to head off this confrontation. "Remember, Chance, you said you wouldn't hit him."

"No, I won't hit him," Chance said as he dug a thumbnail into Workman's wrist, forcing him to turn his shirt loose. But as quickly as he spoke, he saw in the man's eyes trouble that was hell-bent on coming his way. It was a trouble he had never sidestepped in his life, and likely never would. "The hell I won't," he growled as he hit Workman in the face, driving him back into his cohorts.

All sorts of things began to happen then. Chance, grabbing Workman by the shirt with both fists, pulled him off of his friends, who had staggered back a good bit too, and pushed him toward the door. Before Workman could regain his footing, Chance had hit him twice, making the man stagger back, continually off balance and working his way toward that door. Chance didn't notice it, but by the time he'd gotten Workman to the door, the door had been opened. Out of the corner of his eye, he thought he saw Handy holding the door and ready to close it on Workman. It was precisely what happened when Chance hit the would-be tough twice more, knocking him ass over teakettle out the door, stumbling over the boardwalk and down the steps into the dirt.

Then he remembered that Workman had come into this store with two friends, two men who looked to be well-armed, two men he now had his back to. But he need not have worried. For when he looked over his shoulder, his hand on the butt of his Colt's Conversion Model, there was Wash with his own six-gun in hand. The weapon was trained on the two remaining culprits, who now stood stock-still as they watched Wash slowly shake his head back and forth, as though to do what they had in mind would be a very bad idea, a very bad idea indeed.

"Gentlemen," Lieutenant Callahan said to the two, "for future reference, you might want to remember that, unless it is a beautiful woman, I doubt the day will dawn that anyone has Chance Carston under their thumb. Now, unless you have business on this post, I would strongly suggest that you mount your horses and find someplace else to buy your liquor."

With that, Workman's companions silently left the

sutler's store, although they had none-too-satisfied looks on their faces when they departed.

Handy came out of the shadows, and Chance noticed that the man had a bit of a shaken look about him. It was the kind of look a man might get from seeing a ghost from his past, and it caught Chance's curiosity.

"Say, you know any of those fellas, Handy?" Chance asked as Barney, the owner, poured another drink all around. "You looked kinda—"

"Yeah, I know 'em. I know *all* of 'em."

"In a not too friendly way, I take it?" Callahan asked.

Handy glanced at the officer, Chance, and Wash. "It's a long story. Mebbe someday I'll tell you 'bout it."

CHAPTER

★ 8 ★

Lieutenant Callahan met the three of them the next morning at daybreak, shortly after he and the rest of the camp stood reveille formation. He escorted them to the officers' mess tent and seated them at a table with himself.

"It's a different cook on duty this morning," he said to Handy and Chance, who seemed to be looking about for the hard-charging cook they had encountered yesterday. "Don't worry, no one is going to give you any trouble." This last was directed toward Handy in particular.

"Thankee, suh," Handy said with an obedient, humble nod of the head. You'd have thought he was still a slave, Chance thought, the way he was acting.

After eating, Lieutenant Callahan excused himself to go to the finance office, where he would draw a check in the amount of three hundred dollars in payment for the mustangs the Carstons had delivered last night. He had gotten so confident of receiving good stock from them that he hadn't even looked over the stock, except for one brief going-over toward dusk last night. The fact of the matter was, he hadn't received any lame or useless mounts in the time he had known the Carstons. As he left the mess tent, Callahan instructed the three to meet him at the corrals so they could give the mustangs a closer look, "just for the record."

Chance, Wash, and Handy made their way to the corrals, nearly surprised to see all of the horses still there. As feisty and mean-spirited as some of the mounts had been, it was bewildering to see that they would actually consent to being corralled without trying to jump the fence and escape to freedom. The three of them were counting the herd a second time when they were approached by a brazen-looking sergeant major, the kind who had likely been in the army for a good twenty years and was looking forward to the next twenty. It was who was with him that Chance didn't like.

It was Workman and his friends. Workman looked a bit battered, but in walking condition just the same. Chance had a notion that if you gave the man the opportunity to go at it with bare knuckles, why, he might not do too bad a job of defending himself. The basic problem the man seemed to have was that once he got knocked for a loop—such as Chance had done to him last night—he had a real hard time recovering himself. And that was dangerous for a man with a big mouth, which was exactly what this Workman character had.

"There they are, Sergeant Major, right there,"

Workman was saying as the four of them walked toward Chance, his brother, and Handy. "That nigger there, he's the one I come after."

"I don't hold with that kind of talk, Workman," Chance said before the man was even close to him. He spoke loud enough for all to hear him, no doubt about it. "This man's working for me, and you won't call him that, not in my presence. Understand? Or did you forget last night?"

Workman started to run his mouth again, but the sergeant major, whose name was Shaughnassy, cut him short. "I wouldn't go using defaming language hereabouts, Mr. Workman, were I you," he said. "No, sir, not even if you're feeling that way."

"And why not?" Workman asked defiantly, all full of himself and blustery. But he had nothing on Sergeant Major Shaughnassy, who knew how to deal with his type.

"Why not indeed, man! I'll tell you why not. Because of the memories I have of me dear departed papa and mama, that's why. Come to this country after the potato famine of 'forty-six, and got shunned near as bad as me black friend here." Pausing to catch his breath, Shaughnassy stepped closer to Handy, placing a firm hand on the black man's shoulder, as though to relay friendship. Suddenly, the big Irishman's face turned into a scowl filled with hatred. "Because I've never cared for such lowlife terms as *nigger* or *mick,* you see. Face it, old sod, you're out of your league here." Shaughnassy gave a pleasant smile to the Carstons and Handy. To Workman, he said, "Now, why don't ye explain yourself in a more civilized tone, one we can all understand, me good man."

"Perhaps I should handle this, David," Abe Forrest

said as he stepped forward. Forrest was the city marshal of Panhandle, and Chance recalled that he hadn't been with Workman the night before. Still, he appeared to be a man to be reckoned with, although not as full of bluster as Workman. Forrest seemed to be calmer, to have more sense. "It's like this, Sergeant Major," he continued, "we want this man, Handy Partree, back in my town for the murder of Ron Gentry."

"And who might Ron Gentry be, might I ask?" Shaughnassy said in his most civil manner, trying to ingest the matter as best he could. This was, after all, as close as they were likely to see the big Irishman come to anything resembling tact.

"Ron Gentry worked for David Workman," Forrest explained, filling in the information about the fight Gentry and Handy had been in, and the resulting gunfight that took place, supposedly between Henry Morrison, Handy's boss, and Gentry.

"That's about the way I heard it, Marshal," Chance said, speaking up for the first time since Workman had come charging out toward them. "It was Henry Morrison—a good friend of mine, by the way—who had the shootout with Gentry, and they both wound up killing one another."

"My, but news of these gun battles travels fast, doesn't it?" Shaughnassy commented, as though a spectator taking in the whole conversation. And perhaps he was. "Near as fast, I dare say, as Pickett's charge."

"What I'm wondering, Sergeant Major," Chance continued, speaking to the one man who seemed to have a hold on things, daft as he might seem at times, "is how they're figuring Handy in this thing."

"We have a witness in my town who will swear that

it was Handy Partree who was shooting at Ron Gentry just as much as Henry Morrison," Marshal Forrest said, finally asserting his authority.

"You don't say." Shaughnassy was either acting the buffoon or playing this part for all he could get; Chance wasn't sure which. "I'm truly amazed."

"Don't matter what happened or how it happened, Marshal," Wash said. Suddenly, he wasn't so shy.

"Ah, and the younger generation will speak now," Shaughnassy said, bowing to Wash. "Let's get everyone in on this."

"Unless I'm mistaken, that's the badge of a *city marshal* you're wearing, right?" Wash asked Forrest. There was a good deal of patience in his voice, indicating a definite difference in the manner with which he approached a situation, as opposed to his sometimes hotheaded brother.

"Yes, that's right," Forrest admitted with a bit of testiness. Perhaps it was because he knew what Wash was leading up to. "What's your point?"

"Well, mister, my pa's a marshal, a city marshal *and* a federal lawman," Wash pointed out. "And I've worn the badge of a deputy a time or two my own self. What I'm getting at, friend, is that any man who knows a lick about the law knows that your badge and authority ain't worth buffalo chips once you leave your fair city. Now, if you was a federal lawman, it would be a different story."

Abe Forrest gave an I-told-you-so glance to David Workman; any desire to throw his weight around as a lawman had been diminished by Wash's words.

"Well, I must tell you, lads, this is all very interesting," Shaughnassy said. "Why, it almost sounds as though we'll be needing a lawyer right soon if this mess gets any more complicated. And God help us, lads, if we get to that stage, for I've a hateful disposition against that breed who call themselves lawyers. Scourge of the earth, they are. Worse than red men, I say.

"But we're all sensible men, aren't we?" he continued, taking in the lot of them as he spoke. "And we should be able to straighten this out betwixt us, shouldn't we? Now, let's see what we have here." Briefly, Shaughnassy surveyed the men about him and nodded. "A real dilemma, isn't it, gentlemen?"

"What do you mean?" Wash asked, a slight look of confusion about him.

"Well, look at it, lad. A lawman with a badge that ain't worth pinning on, a flannel-mouth who has no proper knowledge of the English language, and orators galore with opinions so diverse you could hardly believe such brains was gathered in one place. And last but not least, a man who is accused of a crime but ain't spoke up once for himself. Now, isn't that modesty for you? Or is it guilt? One could never be sure, I suppose."

"Sergeant major," Chance said with a disbelieving shake of his head, "just what are you getting at?"

"Well, old sod, it's like this. I've got many a responsibility as the top enlisted man on this post. Now, me black-skinned friend here, why, I've never met him before in me life. Same thing with the marshal. And Mother always said to treat a man right until he gives you reason to treat him wrong. That she said.

"On the other hand, you Carston boys and these other wags, well, let's just say your reputation has preceded you." The sergeant major was well aware of

65

the amount of mustangs the Carston brothers had contributed to this post in the past two years, and was as grateful as anyone with a horse to ride could be.

"And how do you figure that my reputation has preceded me?" Workman asked in a growl. He too was tired of listening to this long-winded Irishman. "I don't figure that I've ever been this far south before."

"True, lad, true. But you were here last night and had a bit of a fracas at our sutler's store, I'm given to understand," Shaughnassy said with a mischievous smile. "Lieutenant Callahan, he likes to keep me informed, you see."

"And?" Where Abe Forrest seemed well in control of his temper, David Workman was about to lose his.

"Well, one of me great responsibilities is making sure the riffraff are kept off the post. Can't set a bad example for me soldier boys, can I?" Shaughnassy said. "Now, what I want you to do, Mr. Workman, is give your horses one last watering as a courtesy of your local cavalry unit, mount them, and leave me fair post. And take those two clods hanging on your shirttails with you," he added, indicating the two ruffians who had accompanied Workman to the sutler's store the night before.

Frustrated, Workman was about to go when he stopped and turned to face Handy. "I'm not through with you yet. Believe it," he growled.

"Oh, Mr. Workman, one last thing," Sergeant Major Shaughnassy said with a smile. When the so-called tough caught his glance, he said, "I've considered the Carston boys personal friends of mine for two years now, so I'd take it as a personal affront to me honor if you was to harm them." His smile broadened, and so did the mischievousness about him, as he added,

"Naturally, I'll extend the same courtesy to their friend, Mr. Peartree."

In the two years that Chance and Wash had been coming to this post, neither one could remember speaking any more than half a dozen words to the sergeant major when they had brought in a herd of mustangs, large or small. Now, all of a sudden, they were lifelong friends. But if that suited the situation, so be it.

"Is something wrong?" Lieutenant Callahan said, approaching them.

"Oh, nothing, nothing at all, sir," was Shaughnassy's reply as he rendered a crisp salute to the young lieutenant. "I was just giving travel directions to these men. That's all, sir."

"Well, good, Sergeant Major." Callahan handed Chance a check in the amount of three hundred dollars. "This ought to hold you over for another six months. Not that I want to wait that long to see you again. Whenever you want to get me some more of those mustangs, I'll be more than willing to take them off your hands."

"Fine, Lieutenant," Chance said, and folded the check, placing it in his pocket. "We'll be on our way, then."

While the Carstons and Callahan were saying goodbye, the sergeant major took Marshal Forrest by the elbow and guided him off to the side.

"There is one thing, Marshal," he said in a lowered tone of voice.

"Oh?"

"Why, yes, me good man. While you're here, just don't forget that I'm the top dog on this post, so your badge and any fantasies you might have about tossing your weight around, well, they mean less than prairie dust. Have a pleasant day, sir, and a safe trip, wherever it is you'll be going," he said, leaving the marshal somewhat awestruck.

Shaughnassy found Handy alone over by the corral. He seemed to have a good many mixed emotions boiling up inside of him, the sergeant major thought.

"I don't know what it is you've done, lad, or even *if* you've done it, but however it turns out, Godspeed to you and good luck," he said in a sincere tone.

"Thankee, suh," Handy said humbly when Shaughnassy offered his hand.

"Please, son, don't embarrass me by calling me *sir.*" The sergeant major smiled. "I work for a living, you know."

CHAPTER
★ 9 ★

While Sergeant Major Shaughnassy was straightening out David Workman at Fort Griffin, Ella Mae had nearly finished collecting the dirty linen from the bedrooms in use, replacing them with clean white sheets. As always, she had come to work early, eating her morning meal in the kitchen, then setting about her work as a maid before the sun had even risen. Some days she liked her work, some days she didn't. But one thing was for sure. No one could ever fault Ella Mae for being less than a hard worker, something she had already impressed Margaret Ferris with, even after only one week's worth of work at Ferris House.

She had arrived in Twin Rifles almost a week ago to the day, and what a day it had been. Old Blacksnake Hank, the stage driver who stopped in Twin Rifles twice a week, had pulled his stagecoach to a halt in front of Ferris House, just like always. He was in the habit of informing his passengers that they had all of half an hour to get a meal at Ferris House if they so desired, while he hooked up a fresh team of horses for the next leg of their journey. But after jumping down from his box, he'd opened the coach door and gotten halfway through his spiel before he noticed that Ella Mae was the only passenger on this trip.

"Oh, near forgot," he'd mumbled to himself. "This is as fer as your ticket goes, ain't it?"

Ella Mae had smiled as politely as possible, trying not to act embarrassed, even if she did feel that way, and said, "Yes, sir. I'm afraid it is. Now, if you'll be so kind as to get my bags for me . . ."

As her voice trailed off, Hank had found himself frowning, almost sure he had heard her speak what passed for perfect English out here. No accent, no drawl, nothing like he was used to hearing the coloreds speak. "Lordy, ma'am, you speak words better'n I could ever hope to," he'd commented as he tossed down her luggage.

"I hope so, sir," she had responded in a voice filled with pride. "Someday I'm going to teach school."

"Well, more power to you if you can make a go of it, missy," Hank had said. Then, tipping his hat, he'd boarded his stagecoach and headed for the livery, where a change of horses awaited him.

"Can I help you, ma'am?" It had been Margaret Ferris who had met her as she entered Ferris House.

After Ella Mae ordered a meal, the owner and proprietor of Ferris House had sat down to chat with her. With just as much pride as when she'd spoken to Hank, Ella Mae explained her plans to be a teacher to Margaret.

"That's fine, my dear," Margaret said when Ella Mae was through talking. "But tell me, how are you going to make a living until school starts again?"

The question had caught Ella Mae off guard, and she had to think hard and fast for an acceptable answer. After all, this was the summertime, an aspect she hadn't even thought about when she'd left the plantation. No, she had simply wanted to get away then, wanted nothing more than to be gone from that horrible place, that horrible man.

"I'm afraid I hadn't thought of that," she said with a sheepish smile. Then, after a moment's pause, she added, "Would there be many jobs for a woman in your town?"

"Not many that I can think of," Margaret replied. At least the woman had been honest with her, Ella Mae thought, hadn't talked down to her, as some would. "If you don't mind my asking, do you have any savings, anything you can live on until you get a job? Until school opens?"

Ella Mae slowly shook her head. "After the fare for the stagecoach, I have only twenty dollars left." With those words out, she had dug into her purse and pulled out the remainder of her money, a lone twenty-dollar gold piece, and placed it on the table before her.

Margaret could tell she dearly didn't wish to part with that last money, not even the thirty-five cents the meal would cost. With a smile, she pushed the coin back toward Ella Mae and said, "Let's just call this your welcome meal. No charge."

Ella Mae hadn't known what to say. In fact, she felt downright flabbergasted. After all, in the environment she had grown up in, not many white folks were to be trusted. This woman, she decided, was either a very decent person or a very good liar.

They had talked for perhaps half an hour more that day, before Margaret had to help her daughter get ready for the evening meal. But by then a lot had been said and a good deal of Ella Mae's living expenses had been worked out—at least for the rest of the summer. Although she didn't tell Margaret Ferris the whole story, Ella Mae did get around to admitting that she had no real idea how she would survive the coming two months. Not on twenty dollars, anyway. With that bit of information out, Margaret Ferris had offered her employment as a maid, her job to help change the linens and help out with the wash and in any other areas the Ferrises might need her assistance. Margaret had stated that all she needed was a hard worker, and in one week's time Ella Mae had proven her worth.

Only a year or two older than Rachel, the two young ladies found conversation easy between them when they had the time to talk. In fact, Ella Mae had gotten to like both of the Ferris women. She had also been introduced to Sarah Ann Carston, whose father owned and operated the only competition Ferris House had as far as meals went. Perhaps the biggest surprise of her week-long stay so far in Twin Rifles, had been the fact that she had liked, truly liked, the women she had met here. And they were all *white!*

Dallas Bodeen was out back that afternoon, chopping deadwood into usable pieces of firewood to be fed to the Dutch ovens and stoves in the Ferris kitchen. The sun had seemed to get hotter all afternoon. Still, if he wanted to keep his room, he had to chop wood each day. He set the axe down and wiped a sleeve across his forehead, coming away with an armful of sweat when he spotted Ella Mae coming out the back door to the kitchen.

"Here, Mr. Bodeen," she said with a pleasant smile, handing him a glass of water. "Mrs. Ferris said you'd probably appreciate this."

Dallas took the glass, held it at arm's length as though to admire it, smiled and said, "Ain't it amazing how philosophers come up with them so-called theories they got?" Then, without speaking another word, he proceeded to drink the water in one long gulp. "You're right," he said when he handed the glass back to her, "I do appreciate it."

"What did you mean about the philosophers, Mr. Bodeen?" she asked, a curious look about her.

"Why don't you call me Dallas, ma'am? Everyone else does."

"If that's what you prefer."

Dallas smiled at her. "That's what I prefer."

"Now, tell me about the philosophers."

"Oh, them." Dallas chuckled. "Run across a couple of fancy words one time that was used to describe a body's disposition. *Oppty-mist* was one, a *pessy-mist* was t'other. Now, it seems that the way you tell these two apart is by a glass of water."

"A glass of water?" Ella Mae said in disbelief.

"Yes, ma'am. A half a glass of water, to be exact. Seems this oppty-mist fella, he looks at half a glass of water and claims it's half full. The other fella, the pessy-mist, he does the same thing and claims it's half empty." Again Dallas chuckled. "Don't that beat all?"

"And which are you, Dallas? An optimist or a pessimist?"

"Well, ma'am, I reckon that's where the rub lies. You see, I give some thought to that, yes, I did."

"And?"

"I looked up some more of them big-time words

73

and they definitions and I do believe I found me the right one."

"Is that so?"

"Yes, ma'am. You see, I ain't neither. Closest I can figure is, I'm a *realist.*"

"And how is that?"

Dallas ran a sleeve across his forehead again, glancing at the sun in the western sky when he was through. "In heat like this, ma'am, I don't care if that glass of water is half empty or half full. By George, it's a half a glass of water and I'm a-gonna drink it!"

Ella Mae laughed aloud at the man as Dallas smiled back at her. The old mountain man had always enjoyed seeing others laugh at his tall tales.

"Tell me something, ma'am," he said when the laughter died. "You really think you'll make a go of it as a schoolmarm out here?"

She smiled back at him. "I'm certainly going to try. Why do you ask?"

Dallas shrugged. "I reckon you come a ways, ary you can do that. If you know what I mean."

"You mean because most people with my color skin are usually pretty ignorant?" she said in a tone that demanded an answer.

"If you say so, ma'am." Dallas had learned a long time ago about getting into disruptive arguments with women of any color, and had the good sense to let her think what she wanted. When she was apparently satisfied with his answer, he added, "I reckon I'd better get back to this wood pile, ma'am." He smiled and picked up his axe. "Thanks for the water and the easy company."

"Dallas?" Ella Mae said as she climbed the stairs to the kitchen door.

The Stranger from Nowhere

"Ma'am?"

"Why don't you call me Ella Mae? Everyone else does."

"I'll do that, ma'am. I mean, Ella Mae."

The smile each gave the other was an indication of a friendship to come.

CHAPTER
★ 10 ★

They traveled almost forty miles that day. The trail back to Twin Rifles wouldn't be that hard to ride, basically because they didn't have the herd of mustangs to deal with along the way, as they had coming up to Fort Griffin. Of course, there is something about having a check in your pocket for three hundred dollars that has a comforting effect on many a man. It makes the average man feel like practically everything is enjoyable in life. But Chance Carston wasn't quite your average man, never had been. Every once in a while, as they rode, he would glance over at Handy Partree. To his mind, there were still questions that needed answering, and Chance wasn't much on being held in the dark on things.

There was still an hour of daylight left when Chance

pulled up in front of a fair-sized water hole, looked about him, and said, "We'll camp here tonight."

"What?"

"Yeah, what for? They's still a—"

But Chance cut Handy off. His gaze was direct and hard at the black man as he said, "You mentioned a story this morning that was going to take a while to spit out. I'm just making sure you've got enough time to tell it before the fire goes out tonight."

"I see." Handy came to the realization that, like it or not, he was going to have to tell the Carstons the whole truth about what had happened to him in Panhandle and why that marshal was after him. And David Workman's part in it.

Some boiled beef that the mess sergeant had cut up for them would serve for the evening meal, along with some beans and coffee. Having a biscuit to go along with the meal would have been a luxury right now. But Chance, who usually ate the most of the three of them, didn't complain, for he knew that tomorrow night they would be eating in Twin Rifles. And it didn't really matter where you ate, at the Porter Cafe or Ferris House, the food was downright tasty compared to even Wash's cooking.

For the most part they ate in silence as the sun made its way closer to the western horizon. Still, it didn't take all that long, and Chance thought Handy was getting a mite edgy toward the end of the meal.

"I reckon you likely wantin' to hear a story of sorts," Handy said when he set down his plate.

"As many as it takes," Chance said, putting down his own plate and pouring the rest of the coffee evenly among the three of them. He was all business now. "You see, Handy, it's bad enough when I've got some mean cur tailing me. But I get more than a bit skittish when there's a man toting a badge with 'em."

"I understand." Handy sounded sincere enough. So far.

Chance mulled over a thought in his mind before continuing. "Remember what I said about a man standing by his work hands, even if they were wanted by the law three counties over?" he said, cocking an eyebrow in Handy's direction.

Handy nodded. "Yessuh."

"Well, I'm one of those kind of men, Handy. I'll stand beside you, not behind you. But I like to know what kind of a game I'm being dealt into before I start betting the house on my next move."

Wash had apparently caught on to what his brother was getting at, and said, "That's right, Handy. No one likes to play against a man who's dealing from a marked deck."

"And you want the whole truth before Mr. Workman come afta you, that right?" the black man said.

Chance nodded. "I'm all ears."

So Handy told his story. All of it.

To a point, what everyone had seen on the streets of Panhandle between Henry Morrison and Ron Gentry was exactly what had happened. Words had been exchanged between both men, and they had taken to drawing pistols to settle their argument. Gentry, who had been faster, had put the first slug in Morrison's chest, knocking him backward. But Henry Morrison was a tough man too, and had drawn his own revolver, shooting Gentry in basically the same manner, in the chest. Gentry's second shot had also hit its mark, hitting Morrison in the chest, not far from his heart, by the looks of it. What people didn't see was the fact that Henry Morrison's second shot had gone wild, being fired slightly over Gentry's left shoulder as he himself fell to the ground, dying. Still, Ron Gentry had indeed died of a second wound in the left side of his chest. And everyone had assumed it had come from the gun of Henry Morrison.

But that wasn't true. Not entirely. Here is how it happened.

As soon as the owner of the general store had pushed his way past Handy, on his way out to what looked to be shaping up as a gunfight of sorts, Handy had ducked back inside, momentarily disappearing within the store. Henry Morrison had been a good friend to him over the past three years, and Handy knew he had to do something to help the man out. Something! The only thing that came to mind was the rifles he saw in the rifle rack next to the side door of the store. He grabbed the nearest one, a lever action of one kind or another. A Henry? A Winchester? He wasn't sure. All he could recall was that there was an open box of shells in the drawer below and that he had grabbed two or three, punching them into the rifle's magazine as he rushed out into the alley.

He had only to take three big strides to get the full view of what was taking place on the main street, and it was about then he heard the first shot from Gentry's six-gun. Henry Morrison staggered back as his gun went off next. By the time Gentry had fired his second and fatal shot, Handy was taking a stance, throwing the rifle to his arm and taking aim. It was when Morrison was about to fire his second shot, the one that was misdirected over his opponent's shoulder, that Handy fired the rifle.

Without a second look he'd known that he too had

hit his mark, and quickly rushed back into the general store, placing the rifle in its place on the rack. Then, calmly walking toward the front door in long strides, he rushed out front to the dying body of Henry Morrison.

"If anyone knew it was me killed Mista Gentry, I reckon it was Mr. Morrison," Handy said as he finished telling his tale.

"How's that?" Wash asked, totally enthralled in the man's story.

Handy squinted, as though looking off, far away, perhaps seeing what he was looking for in the past. "It was Mr. Henry, he give me the durndest look, like he knew. Yeah," he repeated softly, "he knew."

"Any idea what you just did, Handy?" Chance asked.

"What?" At the moment, the big black man didn't seem to know or care. It had been a strain on him, telling that story. Chance had the notion he might have been reliving it every day since it had happened.

"You just confessed to a murder."

"Huh?" Handy said in disbelief. Then, "No, I was protecting my boss, Mr. Henry. Thas what I was doin'."

Wash shook his head. "Not if it happened the way you said. It happened that way, we should, by rights, be taking you in to the nearest lawman for the murder of Ron Gentry, whoever he was."

"He was Mr. Workman's foreman, is who he was," Handy said bitterly, a hate-filled look now on his face.

"What was he to you, Handy? What would make you want to protect Henry Morrison against such a man?" Chance asked, patiently probing the man before him in much the same manner Will Carston would with one of his suspects. It wasn't often that it happened, but when it did, Chance could act like a first-rate lawman, almost as good as his father.

"Mr. Gentry was a evil man, the evilest I eva knowed," Handy said in an vindictive tone.

"Oh? And how would that have come about?"

Handy studied his half-filled coffee cup, took a sip, discovered it was nearly cold, and tossed the remaining contents into the sand at his feet, forming a small puddle of mud.

"Before the war, during the war, I was a slave for Mr. Workman, working fields mostly," Handy said, his tone now filled with anguish at the thought of his former status. "Mr. Gentry, he liked to keep the nigga in his place, I reckon. Beat us eva reason he could find."

"How so?" Wash asked.

"I showed you brother deese," Handy said, unbuttoning the front of his shirt and showing Wash the scars on his chest, the ones he had briefly shown Chance back at Ferris House. Wash let out a low moan at the sight of the thick pieces of scabby flesh. Obviously, they had never been attended to properly.

Chance nodded. "It's a sight I won't forget."

Now Handy stood up and pulled his shirttail out of his pants, pulling one arm out of a sleeve and letting it dangle at his side. "What I didn't show you was dis," he said, and turned about so his back was to the Carston brothers.

Chance had never been one to impress easily, but you could tell that what he saw of Handy's back was something he would never forget either. "Lordy," he said in a soft voice filled with awe.

There were twice as many scars on Handy's back as there were on the front of his chest. Thick, jagged, and ugly, they were a sight that was hard to take, even for the staunchest of men, including Chance. But adding to the hideous sight were what looked like several knife cuts and a couple of bullet wounds.

"Not even Chance can claim that ugly a body," Wash said, sadly shaking his head. "This Gentry, he did *all* of that, did he?"

Handy slowly nodded as he turned and put his shirt back on. *"All* of it. Eva las' one of dem."

Chance was puzzled. "Why'd you wait so long to kill the sonofabitch?"

"Mr. Henry, he say no. Say he take care of me, to let him know were dey trouble. And he did." The death of Henry Morrison had meant a lot to Handy Partree. He had lost more than just a good boss, he had lost a good friend, too. And it showed now in his face, which had taken on the saddest look you could imagine. "De one time I try ta hep him, I couldn't." Apparently, Chance thought, the man figured that even on his dying day, he couldn't help the man who had become his best friend.

"Don't worry, Handy," Wash said, standing up and giving the man a supportive slap on the shoulder. "I don't think either Chance or me is gonna turn you in for anything." To his brother he added, "What do you say?"

"Not hardly," Chance said, hoping Handy felt some kind of relief with that knowledge.

"I 'preciate it."

"Actually, Handy, I wouldn't worry about them proving much of a case against you," Chance said as an afterthought.

"How's that?" his brother asked.

Weaponry was Chance Carston's field of expertise if ever he had one, and he put that knowledge to use now. "How's the town doctor, Handy? Real thorough one, is he?"

Handy chuckled to himself. "He work on da bottle more dan he do people."

"A drinker, huh?"

Handy nodded silently.

"What's your point, Chance?" Wash asked, intrigued.

"Well, if my guess is right, that doctor likely pronounced Henry and that Gentry fella dead on the spot and called that his coroner's inquest, then went back to pulling on the contents of a bottle."

"True."

Chance pulled out his Colt's revolver. "Most of these cap and ball pistols are firing the round .44 caliber bullet," he said. "Only way I can see they could figure anyone else had a hand in Gentry's death would be if they actually dug out the bullets in him."

"What dat prove?" Handy asked, now interested in what Chance had to say too.

"If that was a Henry or a Winchester you pulled off that rifle rack, Handy, they were conical shells that were used, not the round ones like the pistols use. Digging those bullets out would prove there was another shot fired at Gentry from a different gun, most likely a rifle. Until or unless someone does that to Gentry's body, you're pretty much in the clear, Handy, for there weren't any real witnesses to what you did."

"None I know of," the black man said.

"Then I wouldn't worry about it, hoss," Chance said, slapping the man on the arm in a playful manner. With a confident smile, he added, "Like Wash says, ain't neither one of us gonna turn you in for nothing."

CHAPTER
★ 11 ★

Chance only woke up once that night, and that was when Wash gave him a start. In the midst of a nightmare of sorts, his younger brother had sat straight bolt upright, having broken out in a cold sweat. It wasn't so much that he gave off a yell, as some who have bad dreams will, as he was breathing so hard. You'd have thought he'd been running for his life, like some of those stories Dallas and Pa told about their younger years in the Stony Mountains. Being chased by grizzly bears and all.

"Bad dream," had been Handy's only comment when he too had been awakened by Wash's movements and heavy panting. He hadn't even bothered to glance at Chance, who was sitting up too, giving his brother the strangest stare, but instead had rolled over and pulled his blanket up over his shoulder and gone back to sleep.

"Yeah," Chance had finally said when Wash, apparently not as fully awake as his brother, had laid back down and continued to sleep. Chance had frowned, muttering "Crazy kid" to himself as he too went back to sleep.

Except for that one instance, Chance had slept well. But it was lying there in the predawn light, just before crawling out of his blankets, that he had begun to think about Handy and his situation, especially after what Handy had told them. It continued to plague him even now, with Handy up and about, silently throwing a slab of bacon on the fire while Wash still lay in slumber.

"Had him a bad night of sorts," Handy finally said, referring to Wash as he poured coffee for himself and for Chance.

"So it would seem," was all Chance cared to say about the matter at first. He was silent for a few minutes while he enjoyed that first cup of morning coffee, then said with a frown, "Can't say as I ever seen him like that before."

"It happens." A hint of a smile came to the corner of Handy's mouth as he pulled back a bit of his own past and said, "Cain't tell you how many a us waken wit chills an' shakes in the dark."

"Sounds like you and your people got put on pretty hard, even when the war ended," Chance said, refilling his cup. The smell of bacon in the air had wakened Wash, and the younger Carston began to stir in his blankets.

"Mighty harsh, Mr. Chance, mighty harsh." The grin was gone now as Handy turned the bacon in the fry pan, glancing up only briefly at Chance as he replied.

Wash knuckled his eyes, working the sleep out of them, then silently made his way to the water hole and threw some on his face. Back at the fire, he dug into his saddlebags, fishing about until he found what he wanted. What he produced was three biscuits, tossing one each to Chance and Handy, keeping one for himself. "Don't go sopping up all the grease before I get my share of it, you hear?" he said.

Like nearly all of their meals, this one was eaten in relative silence, not taking more than ten minutes to deal with the slice or two of bacon each had and the biscuit and coffee to go along with it. Not that any of them had ever gotten used to it, but life on the trail usually meant rations in short supply somewhere along the way. A man simply made do with what he had—or didn't have, as the case might be.

"Didn't they have something at the end of the war—some organization or other—that was supposed to help you folks out?" Chance asked as he gulped the last of his coffee and threw the remains into the small fire before him. Small as the amount of liquid was, it made a sizzle as it put out part of the fire and sent the smell of burnt coffee grounds into the air. "The Freeman's something or other?"

Handy nodded, knowing what Chance was getting at. "The Freedmen's Bureau. Oh, yeah. Da white man's way of fixing everything he destroyed in da South. Yeah, I heared a it. Neva did know much 'bout it, 'cept it wan't 'round for more'n a year. Din' do a whole lotta good, eitha." It was plain to see that Handy was getting more and more uneasy about the subject, the more he spoke of it.

"Well, what I mean is—"

"Don' you think we oughta git us a-going now?" Handy interrupted Chance. "Burning daylight, ain't dat what you say, Mr. Chance?" A hardness had suddenly come to his eyes, and it was aimed right at Chance. And Chance knew it.

"Sure," Chance said in an offhand way. "You're right, we're burning daylight."

Still, Chance found himself torn between a good deal of respect for this man and what he had gone through, and the bullheadedness the man could show when he didn't want to discuss something. If you asked anyone around Twin Rifles, they would likely tell you that Chance Carston had the market cornered on bullheadedness. In fact, if you were to ask Chance himself, he would likely admit to it, and with a good deal of pride.

When they had broken camp and were mounted, Chance caught hold of Handy's arm before the man could race off.

"Do me a favor, Mr. Partree?" he said.

Handy glanced down at the firm grip Chance had, then, raising a suspicious eyebrow, turned his gaze to Chance. "Favuh? Mista?" He had indeed noticed the manner in which Chance had addressed him. "What's on you mind?"

"You've seen that ranch of ours, haven't you?" Chance asked.

Handy shrugged, not sure what was going on here. "Yeah. I reckon. Why?"

"Don't look like no plantation, does it?"

This time Handy smiled. "No, suh, it surely don'."

Chance's tone took on a seriousness of its own as he continued. "Well, I ain't no *Mista,* you understand?

I'm just a working man trying to make a go of it, just like all the rest of us this side of the Pecos. You want to call someone *Mista,* that's my daddy's name. Me, I work for a living. You call me Chance." There was a near scowl on his face by the time he finished, saying, "Understand?"

"I see, suh." Handy nodded, apparently more than agreeable to his master's wishes, something he likely had learned long ago and far away.

Wash, speaking up for the first time since he had tossed Chance and Handy their biscuits, had picked up on what it was his brother was getting at. So he too said his piece.

"That's something else, Handy, that *sir* stuff," he said in near as ornery a manner as his brother. "It's got to go. Why, that was all I heard in the Confederacy was 'sir, this' and 'sir, that.' I do believe all of us got sirred out long before the end of the war. Come to think of it, the lot of us would have kept on fighting if it weren't for that damned word. Just heard too much of it. Made us want to lay down our arms toward the end, it did. No, sir. You want to use *sir* or any other of those fancy slave words on someone, why, you use 'em on Pa." Wash paused a moment to catch his breath—he couldn't recall speaking this much this early in the morning—and gave a mischievous glance at his brother as he concluded with, "He sure is old enough."

With a straight face Chance said, "Ain't that the truth? Claims he knew the architect who fashioned them Stony Mountains, he does." This was followed by a definite nod.

"I see." Handy was still trying to please them by being agreeable.

Chance cocked an arrogant eye of his own at the black man as he said, "Neither one of us ever owned a slave, and we don't want you going about ruining our reputation with your *sirs* and *Mistas.*"

"He's Chance and I'm Wash, and that's good enough for the both of us," Wash said.

"If you say so, Wash," Handy replied with a slight grin.

"Good," the younger Carston said, returning the grin. "I'm glad we got that straightened out."

They were about to move on, when Chance found himself held in place by the firm hand of Handy Partree. He frowned at the man, wondering just what was going on.

"There is one thing, *Chance,*" the black man said, giving the man his friendliest smile.

"Oh?" The frown on Chance's face deepened, for he was still confused about what was taking place. All he knew was he didn't have the upper hand, and he didn't like it. "And what would that be?"

"Don't go digging into my past," Handy said, slowly releasing his grip on Chance. "It were a hurtful place to be then, and it ain' got no betta since. It's still hurtful."

Chance stretched his arm out, as though to find out if all of his muscles still worked. Then he said, "Handy, you're almost as subtle as me."

They rode along at a good pace that morning, not as though they were running a race or delivering the mail for the Pony Express so much as three men who were simply riding along with nothing more to do than enjoy the day. And a fine day it had become. There wasn't a cloud in the sky, and the sun, although becoming hotter the higher it got, was enjoyable to the three of them.

But they weren't halfway through the morning when trouble spoiled their day. It came in the form of David Workman and his crew.

"Damn 'em," Chance cursed to himself as he saw them riding up to their position from the far left. "Seen gila monsters that wasn't as persistent as these fools."

"Told you all I'd bring you was trouble," Handy commented as Workman and his gang neared.

"Reckon it's time I let you in on something, Handy," Wash said, keeping his eye on Workman, offhand trying to count the number with him. Six or eight, he thought.

"Huh?"

"My brother ain't been in nothing but trouble since the day he was born. You just ask Pa. He'll tell you. This is the kind of stuff Chance lives for. Why, it's the only thing he likes better than guns and eating."

"Dat a fac'?" Handy said with interest. Workman and his men were almost on them.

"That and how he feels about Miss Rachel." Wash smiled. "But he ain't never gonna admit to loving the woman."

"Shut up!" The tone in Chance's voice was cold and hard, all business now. All fight.

Workman and his men pulled to a stop in front of them. Chance noticed that Abe Forrest was still with them.

"Thought you had better sense than to stick with this mob," Chance said in his most obnoxious tone.

"I won't say Ron Gentry was a tried and true friend of mine, Carston, but these folks seem to be convinced that Handy Partree had a hand in his death," the Panhandle lawman said. He didn't seem to have wavered over his stance on the issue at all, not one bit.

So far none of them had dismounted.

"Still determined to take him in, are you?" Wash asked in as civil a manner as he could muster.

"Damn right!" Once again it was David Workman mouthing off. "We come for the nigger. That—"

"That was a mistake," Chance interrupted. At the same time he spoke, he swung his leg over his saddle horn, unhooked his foot from the stirrup and slid down the mounting side of his horse.

No sooner was he on the ground than he had his balance about him and was headed for David Workman. But Workman saw him coming and raised a boot, sticking it out toward Chance and his face. Chance caught the big piece of leather with both hands, twisted it hard and pushed Workman off the far side of his horse. The flannel-mouth landed with a heavy thud. By the time he was on his knees, on his way to gaining a stance, Chance had worked his way around the horse. He had fought men like this before, and enjoyed beating them to a pulp. But previous experience told Chance that this man had one hell of a hard jaw, and he didn't want to waste a busted fist on him that way. With that in mind, he kicked the man hard in the stomach, brought his foot up again and flat-kicked his shoulder, bowling him over backward, until he lay sprawling on his back. Vomit leaked out the side of his mouth.

While Chance had taken on Workman, two of his henchmen, the same two who had been present at the sutler's store fight, had begun to go for their guns, just like they had in the sutler's store.

"Tut, tut, now, boys," they heard Wash say, and when they looked, just as before, they found themselves looking down the business end of Wash's six-gun. "I thought you'd have learned your lesson by now."

"That ain't fair," Workman managed to mumble in a moment or two, once he'd gotten rid of the vomit in his mouth.

"Fair ain't got nothing to do with it, Workman," Chance said, a confident leer on his face. "I'm up here and you're down there, and that's all that counts. It does to me, anyway."

Out of the corner of his eye Workman saw Handy grinning from ear to ear, and it was a sight he didn't like, not at all. To Chance, he said, "I'll remember this, Carston."

"I hope you do, Workman," the older Carston replied. "Don't seem like anyone's taught you any manners yet in your lifetime. And as flannel-mouthed as I've seen you get, you may be cutting yourself short on that lifetime. Mighty short."

"Just cool off, you two." Marshal Abe Forrest had either decided to take a hand in the situation or was doing whatever he could to show off for the benefit of David Workman. "I came along to see about a man who might well be a murderer needing to be taken in."

"I thought we had that all straightened out back at Fort Griffin," Wash said, curious about what the lawman was getting at.

"Not really, son," Forrest said. "If you think about it, it was your brother and Mr. Workman butting heads that got us all sidetracked back at the fort."

"Well, as far as I'm concerned, it was settled then and there," Wash said, a frown beginning to set on his forehead. After all, wasn't it he who had pointed out to the lawman that the man had no authority in this territory? Had the man forgotten what he had said that quickly? Or was he ignoring it simply because of his youth? The younger Carston could remember more than one case during the war when that had been the case, any words of wisdom he might have had being totally ignored because of his age. And on more than one occasion he had wondered if he might not have been able to save some men, save some lives, had his information been listened to.

"Oh, I remember what you said, son," Forrest continued. "It's just that the sergeant major got real pushy about us leaving the post and all. If he hadn't butted in, why, I think you might have listened to what I have to say. And I mean to say it now. Unless, of course, you've got other plans." This last was said more as a dare than an aside remark.

"We got all day," Chance said, cutting off his brother, for he knew that as calm as Wash normally was, he wasn't about to be pushed around by any man. Ever since he'd returned from the war, Chance had found that Wash was less and less likely to take any sass from anyone, whereas before the war it was a different story. Chance headed for his horse, removed his canteen and took a good healthy swallow before adding, "Just don't take all day. There ain't that much of the day left."

Handy appeared suddenly interested in what this man had to say, for he knew that it surely must be some sort of a setup, some lie to get him in trouble again. The one thing he felt a bit better about today than he might have felt before was the fact that he now had Chance and Wash Carston as friends who would stand by him if the going got rough. And it looked like it just might any minute now.

"Well, it seems Mr. Workman and his boys did some asking around," Forrest said in an even tone.

"Come up with some things that don't seem to add up at all. No, sir."

"Such as?" Chance asked with a frown. The interest in his face wasn't from doubting Handy's honesty with him as much as it was finding out what kind of lies these men would go to in order to take Handy Partree back to Panhandle for trial.

David Workman spit to the side, obviously still tasting the sourness in his mouth. "The old geezer running the general store is what done him in," he growled in a superior manner. "Claims he seen Partree running from the store. Claims one of the rifles in his rack had a mighty warm barrel to it after the shooting was over. So, hand him over."

"Now, whoa there, mister," Wash said, holding a hand up as though to stop the man. "What you're saying sounds almighty iffy to me." He turned to the black man sitting a saddle beside him. "What do you say, Handy?"

Handy chuckled, although it was a nervous one, which even he would admit to. Then, with what must have seemed like forced boldness, he continued to smile as he said, "Cain't be, mista. Jes' cain't be."

"And how's that?" Wash asked. You'd have thought he was a big-time trial attorney, the way he was conducting the questioning. Chance, silent now, found himself suddenly impressed with his brother's manners. Just like the nightmare, this was a part of Wash he hadn't seen before.

"That ol' storekeeper, why, he's big a gossip as most a dah ladies in town," Handy said, still smiling some.

"What's that got to do with anything?" Abe Forrest asked.

"Why, he pushed me clean outta the doorway, soon's he seen they was gonna be a fight. Rushin' out on dah boardwalk, he was. Gotta have him some gossip to share wit dah ladies when dey visit his store," Handy said with a firm nod.

"You say this store man claims the barrel of one of his rifles was mighty warm after the shooting, is that right, Marshal?" Chance asked in his most civil tone. Not that he was feeling that way. He wanted to finish what he'd started with David Workman in the worst way, but knew it wouldn't accomplish an awful lot at the moment. Instead, he chose to deal with Abe Forrest, who, being a lawman, was more likely to tell him the truth of the situation. For a decade before the war had begun, Chance, Wash, and their father had been active in the Texas Rangers. It was because of this that Chance had a more comfortable feeling about most of the lawmen he had dealt with since returning to Texas after the war. On the other hand, there were still those few who were as sorry a specimen as had ever walked the earth. But then, that was a whole 'nother canyon, as Pa would say.

"That's what he claims, yeah," the lawman confirmed. The foggy frown on his face indicated he had no idea what Chance was getting at.

"And how many times was this Gentry fella shot?"

"Twice."

"No," Chance said, shaking his head, "don't make no sense. Way I heard it, Henry Morrison shot Gentry both times. Now, Marshal, I served with Henry during the war, and I'll be the first to admit he wasn't fast getting that Colt of his out, but I never did find a man more accurate at what he shot."

"What did witnesses to the shooting say?" Wash asked. "Anyone claim it wasn't Gentry shot Morrison, or the other way around?"

"No, that's what most of 'em say, all right." There

was a grudging tone in Abe Forrest's voice, the kind that said he didn't want to admit to this fact.

"Just what kind of a rifle are we talking about, Marshal?" Chance said. "A Kentucky long rifle, a Sharps, what?"

"I believe it was a Henry rifle," was the marshal's reply.

Chance shook his head. "Couldn't have been Handy done the shooting you say. You'd have to empty the better half of a Henry magazine to warm up the barrel like you claim it was. Have to put a good six, eight slugs in Gentry's chest to do that, and you'd hear it with no mistake if more than the handful were fired, like I heard tell."

"Face it, Marshal," Wash added. "Unless you've got an eyewitness, someone who actually saw Handy kill this man, why, you haven't got nothing more than circumstantial evidence. That's what I read in one of them fancy back East law books."

"Besides," Chance said with a cocked eyebrow, "I got a notion that even if we did turn Handy over to you, I'd find out somewhere down the trail that he'd been shot trying to escape, and you know *exactly* what I'm talking about, Marshal."

"I say we bes' be gittin' on our way," Handy said. He glanced at Chance and added, "Burnin' daylight an' all, you know."

"Yeah, I think this conversation is over with," Wash said, and pulled his reins to go.

Handy did the same, in a hurry to vacate the area.

Chance followed suit, but stopped halfway through the movement. As his horse came to a standstill, he slowly lifted his Colt's Conversion Model from its holster, letting it drop loosely back into position. It was his way of making sure these men knew he was talking business.

"There is one other thing you people want to remember," he said in a hard, even voice.

"What's that, Carston?" Apparently, the marshal from Panhandle didn't care to be intimidated any more than Chance, for he did his best to sound tough as nails.

"You figure on taking Handy back to your town, dead or alive, you just remember you'll have to deal with me and my brother to do it." It was all Chance had to say; all he needed to say to let them know his intentions.

Without even looking back, he wheeled his horse away, following Handy and his brother on their trek back to Twin Rifles.

CHAPTER
★ 12 ★

In March of 1865 the United States Congress established the Bureau for the Relief of Freedmen and Refugees. It was originally to be in existence for only one year. Consolidating several departments that had been formed earlier, it soon became known as the Freedmen's Bureau, its purpose in part being to oversee the welfare of former slaves. This responsibility also extended to several thousand white refugees from the South who were fed and clothed from the warehouses of the federal government.

By the end of the war the Freedmen's Bureau had become established in nearly all of the southern states. Through the bureau, not only the government but a good many volunteer relief societies began to assist the black men and women to adjust to life in a free society. Many of them, after all, had known nothing but a life of slavery until the end of the War Between the States. Many discovered that the Freedmen's Bureau was not only a step toward independence but a guardian of their civil rights among white southerners who were moving quickly to enact a series of what became known as "Black Codes."

These black codes did little more than relegate the slave to his former status, rather than enable him to participate in society as a free person. Under many of these black codes, a black man could not vote or hold political office, much less serve on a jury. Blacks were barred from owning a firearm of any type. In order to travel, a black man had to have a residency pass, which restricted his travel limits. In general, he was consigned to treat the white man as a superior being, just as he had been forced to do in his slave status.

But the Freedmen's Bureau helped the black man— and woman—to deal with such adverse laws. The bureau helped them find jobs, set a proper and decent wage for them, as well as terms of labor contracts, and settle them on public lands under the provisions of the Homestead Act of 1862. Often promises of forty acres and a mule did not materialize, largely due to mismanagement and lack of proper funding.

However, Major General Oliver O. Howard, an honest and quite religious man, was appointed commissioner of the bureau from its very inception. And if he accomplished little else, he did manage to establish an extensive system of schooling for the blacks working their way into a productive society. Many had little if any education as slaves, and this system took great strides in making the black man and woman a useful entity in otherwise white communities.

Where Handy Partree didn't know much about the

Freedmen's Bureau, Ella Mae had made it her business to know quite a bit about the organization. Although her reading and writing abilities were limited at the end of the war, she did have a great desire to make something of herself now that she was a free woman—so to speak. It was with the help of the Freedmen's Bureau that she had attended a school set up near the Alabama plantation she had worked on as a slave. Mr. Easton, the white man who managed the slaves on the plantation before and during the war, would never have allowed her to attend school were it up to him. He had never stated it in so many words, but Ella Mae had always suspected that he strongly believed that an education was a dangerous thing for a black to have. But she had persevered through his hateful words and looks and graduated second in her class. She never forgot what her teacher had told her, that she had a great deal of potential to be successful in this world.

Finally, after putting up with more than she thought she should have to, Ella Mae had packed her things, gotten a ride into town, purchased a stagecoach ticket to whatever destination was as far west as her money would take her, and left the plantation. The only notice she gave was a short note tucked under her pillow, notifying Mr. Easton that she could no longer stand his threats and ill manners. Then she had struck out to build a life of her own.

Unfortunately for the Freedmen's Bureau, it was the same as many of the other departments in the Andrew Johnson administration in that it was overflowing with corruption and inefficiency. And men who are inefficient and corrupt can also be men who are capable of having the fear of God put into them.

If nothing else, that was one aspect of human nature that Marcus Easton was well-acquainted with.

Ella Mae was having an enjoyable day. As the days had come and gone, she had found Margaret and Rachel Ferris becoming more and more pleasant toward her, despite the fact that she was little more than a maid. Whenever she had finished her duties, finished cleaning the rooms and changing the linen, she would wander downstairs to the kitchen to rest up a bit before asking the Ferris women what they would like her to do next. Perhaps it was because of this— the fact that she openly asked for more work rather than shirk her duties—that Margaret and Rachel had begun to treat her as one of their own.

One of the ways in which they did so was to point out various townspeople to Ella Mae as they came and went during the noon lunch hour. Often this was done with Ella Mae hiding out of sight behind the swinging door leading in and out of the kitchen, occasionally peeking in on the dining room and its community table.

". . . and that's Mr. Kelly," Rachel would point out, adding, "he owns Kelly's Hardware here in town." She would usually go on to let Ella Mae know any other pertinent information she thought the newcomer should know about Kelly, or whoever it was she was speaking about. Ella Mae had found this information interesting, learning more and more about the people of Twin Rifles. She made a habit of paying attention to these tidbits, storing them away in her memory.

Her day seemed to be getting better and better as she saw Dallas Bodeen enter Ferris House and seat himself at a community table. When he glanced toward the kitchen door, she made sure to open it enough for him to see her, smiling as she gave him a slight wave of the hand. To her surprise, she received a broad pleasant grin and a wave of the hand in return. Silent though they were, she rather enjoyed that form of communication.

"You met Dallas the other day, didn't you?" Rachel said on her way out of the kitchen.

"Yes," Ella Mae said when Rachel returned with an empty serving plate. "He's a very pleasant man. He's quite funny in the way he explains things."

"Young lady," Margaret said in a face filled with mock sternness, "Dallas Bodeen claims to be a *used-to-was* mountain man, and I've found him to be more sarcastic than humorous."

When she marched out into the dining room, a tray of food balanced above her, Rachel tugged at Ella Mae's elbow and whispered, "Mama won't admit to it, but I think she kind of figures Dallas for a romantic old man, too. He helped her out not long ago, you know. Saved her reputation in Twin Rifles."

"Maybe you can tell me someday," Ella Mae said, truly interested in what Rachel was saying.

Rachel shrugged. "It's a long story. Maybe."

As much as she wanted to know how Dallas had helped out Margaret Ferris, Ella Mae knew that it was one of those stories that would come to her when the time was ready and not before. She knew from experience that there was often a time and place for everything in this world, and over the years, she had gained the patience and come to the realization that when her time was ready, certain things would be imparted to her.

"One of our customers is requesting your presence,

dear," Margaret said to Ella Mae with a straight face as she returned to the kitchen area.

At first the words shocked her. "Really?" The only time she could remember a request like this had been those times back in Alabama when Marcus Easton had sent for her in the evening. If she sounded a bit overanxious when she asked "Who?" it was because she was.

"Want to guess?" Margaret was still acting a bit lofty about the whole thing, as though Ella Mae did indeed have a beau requesting her presence. Still, the older woman did seem to have a hint of a smile about her. "It's Dallas," she added when it appeared that the young black woman before her was having a hard time replying, she was that flabbergasted.

"Oh." Ella Mae could furnish only a weak smile, apparently embarrassed at her lack of finesse over the situation.

"Here, if you're going to socialize with him, you might as well have something to do with your hands," Margaret said before Ella Mae could leave the kitchen.

So, with a cup of steaming coffee in her hand, the new—and only—maid for Ferris House made her way to the end of the community table that seated Dallas Bodeen.

"Well, how do, young lady?" Dallas said, smiling at her as she slowly took a seat across from him.

"I feel sort of awkward, taking a seat at the same table as you," she said in a soft voice, her smile taking on a more sheepish nature as she spoke.

"Oh, horse apples, missy," the old mountain man said with a playful scowl, waving aside her worries. "Why, you shoulda spent some time with me up in them Stony Mountains. Recall one time I set down at the fire with a couple of big Crow chiefs and Edward Rose and Jim Beckwourth. They's the two Negra fellers I mentioned the other day. Talk about outnumbered! Here they is, two big chiefs and two big black men, and there I sits, the one and only white man at the fire. I do believe that was the most politest I ever was since leaving Mama's side. Yes, ma'am," he concluded with a smile and a nod.

Ella Mae giggled at Dallas's words, suddenly feeling much more relaxed than she had been. She glimpsed his weathered blue eyes and the joyful look they had about them as he spoke to her. "You're funny, Dallas."

Dallas winked at her. "Only when I want to be. And I find myself wanting to be around you."

The words had an affect on her, and Ella Mae averted her eyes from him, glancing down at the still untouched cup of coffee. She seemed to be shy that way, Dallas thought.

"Besides, I can't do all my talking to you women back at the woodshed now, can I?"

She didn't have to look up to know that he was funning her now, but when she did look up, she saw that she was right. For all she had to hear was the tone of his voice to know that he was in a happy mood. What she didn't know was whether it was because of her presence at the table or if he was that way naturally.

Margaret served Dallas his meal, and their end seemed to be quieter than the rest of the community table. To Dallas this seemed only natural, for he was used to eating and speaking being two distinctly different actions of the human body. You didn't do one when you were doing the other. And Dallas

Bodeen, like many men on the frontier, ate in relative silence.

To Ella Mae this was just as well. It gave her a chance to take in some of the old mountain man's features she had missed out back the other day when he was chopping wood. At that time, she recalled, it was his storytelling abilities that had interested her most. But now, as the old man ate his food in a ravenous manner, she took in the somewhat wrinkled forehead, the skin tanned deeper than any leather she had ever seen. In fact, she was almost certain that it was nearly as dark as her own skin. His hair, on the other hand, could have been bleached white by the same hot sun that had weathered his face. At one time it might have been going through stages of gray, but a good deal of it, she noticed, was now pure white. When the old-timer bent over his plate, as though to inspect it for any food he might have missed, she thought she saw the beginning of a slight bald spot at the very top and back of his head. She observed two fingers on his left hand that appeared to be awfully gnarled, perhaps broken at one point in his lifetime and not having healed properly. It wasn't the first time she had seen such contorted fingers or hands. Many a black man—provided he lived that long—had experienced just the same type of afflictions.

"Didn't know I was worth staring at," Dallas said, bringing her out of a daze.

"Oh, I'm sorry," she said apologetically.

"Don't be." He smiled at her. "Coffee must be almighty cold by now."

Again the sheepish smile. "I'm afraid I'm not much of a coffee drinker. Miss Margaret gave it to me when I came out here, just to be doing something with my hands, I guess," she said, still holding a certain shyness about her.

Dallas decided it was time to bring this butterfly out of her shell.

"Miss Margaret says you plan on being our new schoolteacher," he said, then wiped his mouth and set down the napkin beside the empty plate.

"Yes, sir, Mr. Dallas. Going to start this fall if the good people here will have me," Ella Mae said with what the old mountain man took to be a good deal of pride.

Dallas chuckled, more to himself than anyone else who might notice him. "I'll bet that's gonna set old Hattie to fire, she hears that. Bet your bloomers on that, I do believe."

Ella Mae squinted, clearly confused as to what the man was talking about. "I don't understand."

"Oh, you ain't met old Hattie McNeill yet, have you?"

"I'm afraid not." She smiled politely. "And who might she be?"

"She's the schoolteacher and town gossip, all rolled into one," Dallas said with a wide grin. "Makes you wonder are the kids getting taught the right stuff in school, if you know what I mean."

"And how old might this lady be?" Ella Mae asked, obviously curious about whether she would actually have a job as a schoolteacher in this town.

Again Dallas chuckled. "Old? Why, Hattie's older'n me! And I'm older'n dirt, truth be told. Believe me, Ella Mae, that woman was ready to retire years ago, long afore I ever come to Twin Rifles. Take my word for it."

Ella Mae giggled at his words again, and Dallas began to see more of her that he liked. There weren't an awful lot of women a man could take a liking to and find real humor in. Too bad the rest of the customers had left, for he was sure they would actually like this new addition to the citizenry of Twin Rifles.

But any enjoyment Dallas and Ella Mae might have been having ended right there that afternoon as the Ferris House doors flew open and in walked a tall man in a gray duster. Accompanying him were two other men of somewhat lesser stature, but looking just as determined about something or other that was on their minds.

"Just this side of downright mean," Dallas said to himself when he saw them enter the establishment.

"I hope you realize that if you break the glass in my door, you'll pay for it, mister," Margaret said from inside the kitchen door. She spoke in an authoritative voice, loud enough for all three men to hear from where she stood. But they acted as though they didn't even hear her. Or didn't care. Perhaps both.

What they were interested in was Ella Mae. Dallas never could recall a person of color ever really turning white as a ghost, but it crossed his mind just then that at this moment Ella Mae did look a mite peaked around the face and gills.

"Didn't think I'd come after you, did you, Ella Mae?" the big one wearing the duster said in a booming voice.

"Now, you just pipe down, mister. My hearing's fine as it is," Dallas said with a frown. Already he'd decided he didn't like the man.

"I ain't-talking to you, old man. I'm talking to my Ella Mae," was the big man's reply. A sneer had now appeared on his lips.

Ella Mae's voice trembled with fear as she said, "I ain't yours, Marcus Easton. I was never yours, and

107

you know it." There was a quiver to her lips and tears welled up in her eyes.

If he'd had the time, Dallas thought he might feel sad about the whole situation. Instead, he found himself filled with hate for the way this man was treating Ella Mae.

"Does what he's saying mean what I think it means?" Dallas asked Ella Mae, still seated across from her. Silently, the young maid nodded in the affirmative as tears rolled down her cheeks. But as he saw them, Dallas wondered if they weren't tears of shame more than fear that this woman was feeling. He had a good notion what that could be too.

"I didn't come here to debate nothing, Ella Mae, so you save your education for another time," the big man, who apparently was one Marcus Easton, growled. "Get her, Walt," he added to one of his cohorts, "we've got places to go."

Walt, not quite as tall as his boss, but appearing to be just as ugly and mean, made his way toward the maid. When he was behind her—for she was still seated across from Dallas—he placed both hands on her shoulders and was about to physically lift her from the seat she was in.

"I hate to see good food go to waste," Dallas said as he reached over, grabbed up Ella Mae's coffee cup, now filled with the lukewarm liquid, and tossed it over the maid's shoulder and into Walt's face. Hot or cold, the coffee wasn't something he appreciated having thrown in his face, and he was soon shaking it.

But by the time he was doing that, Dallas had tossed the cup aside, reached up and grabbed one of the man's ears. Giving it a yank, he pulled the man over to the side of Ella Mae, placed his other hand over the second ear, and slammed Walt's face down on the community table. Blood spattered in all directions as the man's nose broke. The old mountain man still had hold of Walt's ears, and he leaned across the table now, holding the man's face directly in front of his own. The man might have been only half conscious, but that didn't stop Dallas Bodeen from speaking his piece.

"Now, you listen to me, you sorry son of a bitch," he growled at the man. "You touch this lady again and it'll be the *last* thing you ever do on God's green earth, cause I'm a-gonna git rid of one more plug-ugly in this world that day. And that's you."

When Dallas dropped Walt to the community table, unconscious, he looked up to see Margaret Ferris holding an oversized horse pistol in her hands. It was pointed straight at Marcus Easton and his second companion, both of whom had begun to pull their guns.

"Mister, I won't have any shooting in this establishment, so you just put that toy of yours back where you had it." Margaret was all business, that was for sure. "My Abel taught me how to use this thing, so I hope you're paying attention."

"I'm surprised you can hold it, lady," Marcus Easton said with a sneer about him.

"Sonny, ary you ain't old enough to have ever seen one, what she's holding is a Walker Colt," Dallas said with a shake of his head that said he couldn't believe the stupidity of the man he was addressing. "Old Sam Walker helped design it, he did. Got us Texas Rangers two of 'em back during the Mexican War.

"What you gotta realize here is that she don't have to hit you when she fires that thing. Why, the concussion alone will kill you. And the rest of us is gonna go deaf from the echo in here, which by my calculations ain't gonna stop for a week and a half." Dallas managed to get that mouthful out with a straight face.

"Now just what is it that's a-going on here?" a figure suddenly appearing in the doorway said. Joshua Holly was the deputy marshal of Twin Rifles, Will Carston's right-hand man. For that matter, he was Will Carston's only man. "Doors a-banging open, glass rattling, why, it can be downright discomforting, it can." He took a quick survey of the situation, the man called Walt lying facedown in his own blood in front of Dallas, the two strangers with their guns half drawn. "Dallas, you telling more of them wild stories of yours? That what got this shindig a-going, you old coot?"

"Don't you go calling me an old coot!" Dallas said, and went on to explain what had happened and how the situation had gotten heated up like it did.

"Enough of this storytelling, gentlemen," Margaret said in a stern voice, the Walker Colt still in her hands and pointed in the general direction of Marcus Easton and his friend. "Deputy, I want this riffraff out of my establishment. I don't need their kind of trouble."

Without another word, Joshua had his own six-gun out and trained on Easton and company. "You heard the lady, gents, you just put the hardware away and git your friend and let's mosey outside a mite and I'll introduce you to the law in Twin Rifles."

When Easton and his cohorts were outside, Dallas walked up to Margaret Ferris and said, "I'm glad you come out when you did, Miss Margaret. Having that gun sure did come in handy."

"What, this?" Margaret looked at the Walker Colt as though it were one of her tools and nothing more. "For your information, this thing hasn't been loaded since Abel died."

The old mountain man's eyes nearly bugged out. "You mean it was empty!" he said in a hoarse voice.

"Of course, didn't you know that?"

He shook his head in disbelief. "Miss Margaret, you're a fine cook, you truly are. But I gotta tell you, there's days you can give a man a scare worse than the entire Blackfoot nation."

Ella Mae watched him as he plunked on his hat and made his way out the door, probably headed to Ernie Johnson's to have a drink and settle his nerves.

With a smile, Ella Mae said to Margaret, "I guess he is kind of romantic, in his own gruff way."

"Honey," Margaret replied in a stoic tone, "he's a man. They all get a streak of that in them once in a while."

CHAPTER

★ 13 ★

The Carston brothers and Handy Partree still took their time getting back to Twin Rifles that last day. It was just that they took their time in a way that was a whole lot more cautious than before meeting up with David Workman and his bunch. To say that they distrusted themselves would have been pure folly. If they distrusted anyone, it was Workman and his men. Even with Marshal Abe Forrest along with them—a man who, Chance grudgingly admitted, seemed on the level as far as knowing his law and being honest and fair with a man—Workman was not to be trusted to mind his own business. Still, none of the three was able to spot the troublemaker that morning on the trail. And neither Wash nor Handy gave much of an argument when, at noon camp, Chance insisted that they continue on their journey, guaranteeing Handy they would be in Twin Rifles within two hours.

"I'll buy you a beer and a steak once we get there," the older Carston brother said, trying to sweeten the pot in his own way. After all, he was carrying a check for a goodly sum of money on this return trip.

Handy chortled, to himself as much as either of the brothers. "Long as we don' run into Workman and his crowd. Two hours can be a mighty long time, you know."

"You're as bad as Wash," Chance said, in what sounded like a disgusted tone. Then, slapping his reins across his horse's rump, he added, "Gonna wind up worrying yourself to death, like them old hens in town."

Then he was gone, riding as though he could care less whether his brother and the big black man were with him or not.

Handy watched him ride off, a confused look about him as he did. "Tell me somepin, Wash."

"If I can."

"Does dat brother of yours have a death wish?"

Wash gave a short laugh before turning his attention to Handy. "It's like this, Handy. I figure Chance will still be bucking the tiger by the time he gets to be Pa's age."

"Hmmph. Eff he live dat long." Wash noticed that Handy's tone had about as much disgust as his brother's had. Then Handy too was gone, riding pell-mell after Chance. Wash brought up the rear.

Chance was right in his estimate that it would take upward of two hours to make it back to Twin Rifles. From where the sun stood, he figured it was close to two o'clock or so as he pulled up to a creek not far from his town.

113

"Surprises me that Workman and his bunch didn't stop us again along the way," he said in an offhand manner as his horse took a drink from the creek.

"Maybe they believed that story you gave 'em and decided to head back home," Wash said with a shrug.

"Tain't likely," was all Handy Partree would say. Apparently, Handy was still expecting trouble of some sort.

"Get us a beer at Ernie Johnson's, put up the horses, and order up a steak over at Ferris House," Chance commanded the other two. "Except Wash. He don't eat no place but Porter Cafe."

"You got that right, big brother," Wash replied. "But if you're actually gonna buy that beer, I'll take you up on it."

"Done." Chance slapped his reins across his horse's backside and was soon on his way to town, pulling up in front of Ernie Johnson's saloon.

"Tell you what," Handy said as they all dismounted. "I'll take these hosses down to Mr. Reed at the livery. I s'pect he wanting to know where I been. 'Sides, them hosses need a drink worse'n you two do. I be back soon's the hosses git took care of."

"Couple of beers, Ernie," Chance said when the brothers walked into the saloon and headed for a table off to the side. It was close to mid-afternoon, and the lunch crowd had come and gone, leaving only a handful of steady drinkers in the establishment.

Ernie Johnson served them their beers, making polite query about where they had been and what they'd been doing, then left. The two brothers sat in silence for five minutes, enjoying their beers, then began discussing what they would do with the money they had just made. Part of it, they both agreed, would go to Handy Partree, who had done a better job than either of them had imagined they would get from the man. It was when Chance yelled out an order for more beer that Wash saw him squinting at some men at the bar.

"Something caught your eye?" he asked when Chance's squint turned into an ugly frown.

"Ain't that Abe Forrest at the bar?" Chance asked in a disappointed tone. It almost sounded as though Chance knew there was a fight coming but didn't want to participate in it, something Wash found uncommon in him.

"You know, I think you're right," Wash replied. It was then he understood the look on his brother's face, for if Abe Forrest was about, David Workman couldn't be far away. And that meant trouble of one kind or another. "And I was just beginning to enjoy my beer," he added in disappointment, knowing that any pleasure he might be savoring here was pretty much gone for the day.

And in walked Handy Partree.

Like anyone else walking into a saloon from the bright sunlight, he had to stand there a moment to adjust his eyes to the darkness. But before he could see who all he was with in the saloon, he was in for a shock.

"You ain't drinking in here, nigger." It took a minute for him to recognize the voice of David Workman, but when he did, his blood ran cold.

"What're you doin' here?" Handy said, a growl creeping into his voice, a scowl to his face. His eyes had focused now, and he took two huge steps past two men at the bar, stopping in front of Workman, who faced him.

"When I said I come to get you, Handy, I meant just that," Workman said with a sneer.

115

"Well, I ain't going, and dat's dat." Handy was opening and closing his fists into big balls, a sure sign that he was ready for a fight.

"We'll see about that, nigger," Workman snarled in what was meant to be a superior manner.

At the Carston table Wash suddenly had a worried look on his face. "Don't look like the odds are too even," he said as he saw one of the two men Handy had passed move behind the big black man. But when Wash started to push his chair back, to go to Handy's assistance, he was stopped by Chance placing a big hand on his wrist, holding him in place.

"You're right, brother," Chance said with a smile as he took in the whole event, "the odds ain't even at all."

The man behind Handy was suddenly in action, pinning Handy's arms behind his back as David Workman proceeded to hit the black man in the stomach three times in a row. But it was almost as though the blows had little or no effect, for Handy only flinched the third time he was hit. Still, the man was quick on his feet. Workman drove his arm back as far as possible, and Handy knew the man was going to hit him in the face. When Workman's right arm shot out at him, he ducked to the side, and Workman hit his own man, nearly knocking him out. Before Handy could break loose of the man's grip, which was weakening, he straightened back up and brought his forehead directly down on Workman's nose, sending blood spurting all over the area. He stomped down on the foot of the man behind him and, as the yell went out, broke free of his grip and grabbed him by his shoulder, hurling him off to the side. He half turned to his right, bringing his arm and fist around and hitting the second man at the bar alongside the head. The man was late getting out of the way and dropped to the sawdust floor, unconscious. Last but not least, Handy let go a walloping roundhouse right that landed square on Workman's jaw. The blow swung the man around before he too dropped to the floor in a less than conscious state.

The man Handy had hurled off to the side wound up rolling over toward the Carston table, not far from Wash. The younger Carston noticed this was one of Workman's men who had gone for his gun at both the sutler's store at Fort Griffin and just the other day when they'd had their run-in with the Workman crowd. He also saw the man again going for his gun. Wash stomped the heel of his boot down on the man's wrist, as though intent on killing an insect. The man let out a yell that could be heard even outside the saloon.

"You know, mister, every time I see you, you're trying to shoot someone," Wash said as he pulled his own six-gun and stuck it in the man's face. "Next time I think I'll just kill you and be done with it."

The man was suddenly silent.

While Wash was taking care of the would-be shooter, Chance and Ernie Johnson had taken matters into their own hands. After all, this was Ernie Johnson's saloon. While the bartender and proprietor of the establishment was fishing around for his .double-barreled shotgun underneath the bar, Chance was on his feet, his Colt's Conversion Model .44 in his hand, cocked and ready for a fight.

"I'm game if you are," he said aloud at any one of the rest of Workman's men, who had been going for their guns but suddenly froze in place.

By then Ernie Johnson had his shotgun out and cocked, ready for business. "Believe me, gents, you don't want to die in my place. All I'm gonna have 'em do is haul your carcass off to the pile of manure off behind Reed's Livery. You'll wind up being picked apart by the buzzards during the day and the wolves who dare come this close to town at night."

It was then Will Carston came through the bat-wing doors, with the look of a man who has been disturbed on an otherwise peaceful afternoon. He gave Wash and Chance the same kind of scowl he used to give them when they were youngsters and he'd caught them in trouble over something. "What kind of trouble have you two started now?"

"Didn't start nothing, Pa," Chance said in his own serious tone, Colt revolver still sighted in on Workman's crowd. "I was just trying to keep my hired hand from getting shot."

"Dat's da truth, Mr. Carston," Handy said, rubbing his right fist into the palm of his left, trying to work out the soreness of it from hitting Workman. He too had found out David Workman had a jaw nearly made of stone.

"He's got it right, Will," Ernie Johnson said, still holding firmly to his shotgun, trained on Workman's men. "The flannel-mouth sitting there, doing all the bleeding, he started the whole thing. The way the rest of 'em was ready to go for their guns, I figure they're the troublemakers."

"All right, gentlemen, put the hardware away," Will said, a good deal of authority in his voice. He made no attempt at trying to hide his U.S. Marshal's badge, hoping any of them wanting to carry on this fight, whatever it was about, would keep in mind what they were getting tangled up in if they did decide to go against his wishes. To David Workman, who was holding an already red-stained neckerchief to his nose, he said, "If this bunch of yahoos belongs to you, mister, I'd strongly suggest that you pay up your bar bill, mount those broomtailed nags I see out front, and say good-bye to Twin Rifles. I won't tolerate troublemakers in my town, and that, gentlemen, is that."

Marshal Abe Forrest, who had been inconspicuously absent from the scene once Workman began to mouth off, now made his way to Workman's side.

"You'll have to forgive Mr. Workman, Marshal," he said in his most tactful manner. "He does have a temper, and at times it can get away from him."

"Then he picked the wrong town for it to get away from him in," Will said with a frown.

To Marshal Forrest, Ernie Johnson said, "Then maybe you'd better explain to him that I'm the one who decides who does and doesn't drink in my establishment. Not some flannel-mouth stranger." Then, to Handy, as though the black man was a longtime friend, he added, "Adam's ale is your poison, ain't it, Mr. Partree?"

Handy's head shot back harder than if Workman had actually hit him in the face, he was that surprised at the way Ernie Johnson was talking to him. Mr. Partree? "Why, yessir, yes it is."

Ernie Johnson went out back and brought back Handy Partree's glass of water.

"Marshal, you seem like a reasonable man," Forrest said. "Actually, what we've come here for is to take a man back to our town, to Panhandle. It's Handy Partree I'm speaking of."

"That right, young man?" Will said to Handy, who was now drinking his water.

"Don't listen to 'em, Pa," Chance said, butting in. This, Wash noted, was very much like his brother.

119

"Me and Wash heard their story a day or so back, and they ain't got nothing but half-baked evidence on Handy. No eyewitness or nothing."

"Is that right, Marshal? My boys hash this out with you, did they?" Will said, giving Forrest a look that was all business.

"Well, yes, I suppose so." Abe Forrest's voice was abruptly lacking in confidence, not to mention authority. "But we still—"

Will, who had taken an interest in the marshal's badge, interrupted with, "City marshal, are you?"

"Yes, but what does that have to do with—"

"Why, everything, Marshal, just everything! You see, it don't matter which direction you come or go in this town. The sign at the city limits says Twin Rifles, *not* Panhandle," Will said. "So you see, Marshal, that hunk of tin on your chest don't mean beans lessen you're trying to look pretty or important. So you just gather up this crew you brought with you and git 'em out of my town."

"I'll do that, Marshal," Abe Forrest said, and began to direct Workman and his men out of the saloon.

"And Marshal?" Will said, when all of Workman's men had gone and Abe Forrest was the only one left.

"Yes."

"I'll check out this shooting you're talking about, and if the man's worth sending back to you, I'll escort him to Panhandle in person," Will said with a nod. "I don't like killers any more than I expect you do."

"Thanks, Marshal, I appreciate it."

When Abe Forrest and the others had left, Will turned his attention to Wash, Chance, and Handy.

"I think the four of us need to have a talk in the not too distant future."

CHAPTER
★ 14 ★

After the confrontation with Workman and his crew, Chance, Wash, and Handy finished their drinks— Handy still had to chuckle at the prospect of calling water a drink in a place like Ernie Johnson's saloon— and left. Outside, Chance gave Handy instructions to head for Ferris House, stating that he would meet him there after he made a deposit at the bank. Wash, of course, left for the Porter Cafe and a reunion, not to mention a decent meal, with his wife, Sarah Ann.

It was Margaret Ferris who showed Handy Partree to a seat, even though it was mid-afternoon and hardly anyone was seated at the community tables, the lunch meal having already been served, the supper meal not yet upon them. In fact, the only person seated was Dallas Bodeen, who seemed to be nursing a glass of water at the farthest end of the community table, the end closest to the kitchen entrance.

"I don't s'pose dis got nuthin' to do wit the fac' dat—" Handy started to say, knowing full well the woman was being cautious, just like all the rest of the white folks he had run into at one time or another. Most of them didn't have the courage to come right out and tell you they didn't favor the color of your skin. Instead, they would guide you to the back table, just in case someone of their own race happened to come through the door and wanted something to eat. Trying to keep their business and maintain peace is what they were trying to do, he had reasoned.

"I'm setting you right back here, Mr. Partree, because, as you can see, I'm between meals right now, with the exception of Mr. Bodeen, who would spend more time sipping coffee in here than being out back chopping his fair share of the wood I'll be needing for my upcoming meals," Margaret said, interrupting Handy. "I dare say that next to drinking coffee, Mr. Bodeen has always had a penchant for gossiping with others. Palavering, I believe he calls it. That, sir, is why you are being seated here." Then, with a furrowed brow and a glare to match, and looking right at Dallas Bodeen, she added, "Besides, he's been bothering my maid more than need be this afternoon."

Then she disappeared, only to reappear within a minute, an empty coffee cup and a steaming pot of coffee in her hands. When she poured and asked Handy for his order, he told her of Chance's promise of a steak once they got back to town.

"Hmph, that'll be the day," Margaret said as she took Handy's order.

"Ma'am?"

"Chance Carston won't pay for any more than he

has to," she said, more as a statement of fact than anything else. Then she was gone, off to the kitchen again.

"What she mean by dat?" Handy asked, still slightly confused.

Dallas chuckled. "I heard her one time when she was really fired up. Claimed that whenever Chance gets up the nerve to ask Rachel to marry him, why, she figures it'll be her and Rachel who will have to buy the rings."

From behind the kitchen door came Margaret's booming voice. "I heard that, Dallas Bodeen. Heard every word of it." When Dallas made no reply—or had better sense than to make such a mistake—she added, "There's wood out back still needs chopping, you know."

"Yes, ma'am," was the old mountain man's response, spoken in much the same manner as a young man acknowledging his stern mother's orders—scared. "I'll be getting right to it. Yes, ma'am. Right to it."

Handy smiled as Dallas gulped what was left of his glass of water and stood up, grabbing his hat off the peg on the wall. "Say, you seen old Harvey Reed since you been back?"

"Yes, sir." Handy nodded in the affirmative, sipping his coffee. "Jes' now. Be goin' to work for him tomorrow."

Dallas smiled. "Good. I'm glad to see things are going well for you."

Dallas had been sitting with his back to the wall, able to see the stairway leading to the second floor of Ferris House, where the rooms were located. Handy had been seated directly across from Dallas, his back to the stairway. When Dallas stepped out from behind the community table, he caught sight of something that pleased him, if the look on his face was any indication. Then his gaze fell to Handy.

"Why don't you sit over here, son," he said, indicating his seat. When Handy looked at him with a curious frown, Dallas smiled and said, "The view's a whole lot better, believe me."

Backing down the stairs, one at a time, was Ella Mae, a straw broom in one hand, a dust pan in the other. Silently, Handy got up and exchanged places, moving his coffee across the table with him. Seated, he realized that he could sit, drink his coffee, and watch Ella Mae continue to dust the stairs to the second-floor rooms. And a pleasurable sight it was. It only took one brief glance at the woman for Handy to say, "I do believe you're right."

Then Dallas excused himself to get back to the work of chopping wood out back of the kitchen.

At the same time Dallas disappeared from the room, Chance entered Ferris House and seated himself across from Handy. No sooner had he taken a seat than Margaret came out, a hefty plate in each hand. She took great deliberation in setting one of the steak dinners down before Handy and one down before Chance.

"How's that for service?" she asked, once she was through bringing out biscuits, potatoes, and an array of condiments, including gravy.

At first Chance was stunned by the woman's behavior, then simply said, "I ain't never complained about your service, Miss Margaret, you know that."

"I know," she said. "The only thing you've ever complained about was not having *enough* food."

Still unable to understand what the woman was getting at, if anything, Chance dug into his food as though she weren't there at all. You would have thought he hadn't eaten in a week, the way he attacked the steak and everything else within sight. Or perhaps he was afraid someone else would come out and lay claim to the piece of meat before he could finish it. Neither the Carston family nor anyone else had ever figured out Chance's reasoning in eating what he did the way he did, and no one ever likely would. All they knew was it was best to stay clear of the man until he was through, the same as when he was fighting or shooting. Food, fists, and firearms seemed to be the three things Chance had dedicated his life to, not necessarily in that order of importance.

When he was through eating, not more than fifteen minutes later, he pushed away his plate, belched, drank the last of his coffee—his cup was immediately refilled by a smiling Rachel—and dug his hands into two of his pockets. Margaret Ferris, he was sure, was likely heaving a sigh of relief to see him actually pay for a meal. He held a combination of gold and silver coins, as well as paper money, in the palm of his big hand. Taking his time to count the money by sight, he picked out a coin and left it on the community table, next to his plate. Nearly all of the bills and several of the other coins he plunked down in front of Handy.

"I figure this is yours, hoss," he said with an appreciative smile. "I'm glad we had you along. Oughta get you going, if sticking around is what you got in mind for Twin Rifles."

Handy looked in wonderment at the pile of money before him, as though he had never seen so much at one time. Or perhaps that he'd never been given that much all at one time. Not if you didn't count the hundred dollars he had taken when leaving Henry Morrison's spread.

125

"Sixty dollars?" he said, his eyes wide.

Chance nodded. "Sixty dollars. I figure you earned it." With a chuckle, he added, "Hell, seeing you draw blood on Workman was worth every cent of that money."

"Told you I wouldn't be nothin' but trouble," was all the big black man would say in reply.

In a more serious tone, Chance looked across the table at Handy and said, "Look, I meant what I said about standing by you. Every word of it."

"I know, Chance. I unnerstan'."

"Good," Chance said, getting up from the table and sloshing on his hat. He was about to head for the door when he stopped and turned back toward Handy. "You know, Pa and Wash and me and even old Dallas, why, we was fighting tough nuts like Workman long before that damned war come along. He ain't nothing new to any of us, so don't you go fretting about him. Whether you know it or not, mister, you've made some friends in Twin Rifles."

Handy nodded in silence as Chance left Ferris House. He knew that it was good for a man to have friends, but at the moment he was wondering what kind of friend Ella Mae would be.

For she was staring right at him.

CHAPTER

★ 15 ★

Where Handy sat wasn't the only place a person could get a view. All the while Handy had been sitting there with that pensive look about him as he listened to Dallas speak, Ella Mae, having spotted him as she worked her way down the stairs to the second story, could see him out of the corner of her eye. And when she saw that he was watching her, she made an extra effort to put a bit more wiggle into her work. Not that she was a tease or anything, for she had found out what that kind of woman got back in this world when she worked for Marcus Easton. But that was long ago and far away, and she wanted to put it out of her mind. Taking in the features of Handy Partree seemed to do wonders to ease her worries.

"You keep staring like that, your eyeballs will drop

out," she said with a mischievous smile when she interrupted whatever it was he was thinking about.

"Sorry, ma'am, I din' mean to." There were times this man was overly apologetic, she thought, and wondered why. Weren't they all supposed to be free now, free to do and say as they liked? It was a question she often asked herself, but thought better of voicing it here and now. This Handy Partree might not have a handle on the answer she had been toying with the past few years concerning freedom.

"No need to apologize. I was staring too," she said instead, a hint of her smile still prevalent about her.

"I din' notice." Still apologetic, still humble.

"Oh, I don't think a man notices much a woman does these days, much as they have on their mind. The men, that is." Handy likely didn't notice that this young lady was treating him just as she would a young child in one of her classrooms. When her words brought no response from him, she added, "I'm going to be the schoolteacher here come fall."

Handy nodded. "I think I heard that."

She stood there in silence for a moment, sizing him up. As big and strong as he was, she was certain that his body contained a number of scars of various sorts. Not many a black man got by without some sort of beating from the master now and again. Had to keep us niggers in line, she thought to herself. He wasn't bad-looking either. Tall and muscular and likely able to take care of himself with a build like that. It crossed her mind that perhaps the shyness and humbleness about him was just an act he put on. Perhaps it was nothing like his real self. In a way, she found herself hoping so, for she had never cared for the shy, withdrawn character of some people of her race.

"Do you know your letters?" she asked, still speaking to him as though he were a student of hers.

But rather than open him up the way she wanted, her words seemed to offend the man. A sudden frown came to Handy as he said, "My, but ain't you da pryin' young woman."

He could have slapped her in the face, his words hit her that hard. "Excuse me," she said, in what was truly an uppity manner, "I was only trying to make conversation." Then she turned about to leave the area. But she didn't get far.

"I know my letters," Handy said suddenly, in a booming voice. When Ella Mae stopped to look over her shoulder, he added, in a considerably lower tone, "I jes' don' know all da words dey makes."

"I didn't mean to get you mad, you know." She had turned full around and was facing him now, standing still and not going anywhere. Although she didn't say it, she was hoping he would take a bit more notice of her.

"Don' reckon I eva took to being questioned all dat much," Handy replied in his normal tone of voice. It was as close as she would ever get the man to apologize to her, and she knew it.

"I guess we're both strangers to Twin Rifles," she said, trying once again to be pleasant.

"Uh-huh."

Maybe he would feel better if she volunteered some bit of information about herself, she thought. Sometimes that worked with people when they were reluctant to talk about themselves. "I went to one of those schools the Freedmen's Bureau opened back East," she said, a hint of pride in her voice. "Got my degree in teaching there."

"You talk edicated," Handy said before pausing in thought. His eyes searched the floor, as though the words he wanted to speak could be found there, then quickly glanced to the side and back to Ella Mae. "Mama taught me da letters. I neva did go to no school, though. Too much work in da fields, so dey always tol' us."

"I could teach you," she said in a suggestive way. "To read better. To talk better."

"Me?" He said it as though to do so would be asking the impossible.

"Sure." She seemed to be suddenly filled with excitement and confidence over the prospect of teaching this man something, anything. "You have to admit, the way you talk now, well, you sound so . . ."

"Ignorant?"

The humble look was now upon Ella Mae as she glimpsed the face of big Handy Partree, not sure if what she was about to say would raise his ire again or not. "As a matter of fact, yes."

"But don' you see, dat's how mos' folk look on me," he said, defending himself. "Jes' some dumb ol' nigger is how dey see me, Miss Ella Mae." With these last words, he seemed to have lost any confidence he might have had. She knew it for a fact when his big body slumped down on the seat at the community table behind him. Perhaps the only good thing about it was that she was now looking the man straight in the face rather than having to look up to him. Lord, but he was tall!

She had to admit to herself that the only thing this big strapping man looked like now was a young schoolboy who had been shamed by something or other and was hurting quite deeply. She also had to admit that she felt stumped. Oh, they had taught her how to handle children in the schoolroom, how to take care of discipline and the actual teaching of the three R's. But she couldn't recall them lecturing about trying to meet the emotional needs of a student. So it took a minute or two of hard thought before she could come up with a possible solution to this problem.

"Handy, your mama taught you manners, didn't she?" It was a question with a foregone conclusion, for she couldn't remember anyone who hadn't been taught how to have manners by their mother when they were a child. It was drilled into you as though you would be the disgrace of the family if you didn't have manners around others. They never did tell you that the underlying reason for the emphasis on manners was to treat the boss man properly once you were old enough to work the fields, or wherever else they had a place for you on the plantation.

Handy half smiled. "Sure."

"Well, if you were to polish up your words and how you use them, and stick to your manners, you'll be as good as any man walking the streets of this town. I guarantee it." She said it with every bit of pride she could muster, partly because she wanted to inspire him, partly because she wanted to get to know this man better, and this might very well be the way to do it.

"How dat gonna happen? You joshin' me, right?" he said in disbelief.

"Simple. I'll teach you how to speak better. Actually, it's not as hard as you may think."

"And what dat gonna do for me in dis town?" he

asked stubbornly. He seemed to be dead set on proving her wrong.

"The people in this town won't think of you as a dumb nigger anymore, that's what."

She sure did have gumption, Handy thought. He'd say that for her. And who knew, maybe she could teach him a thing or two about the English language after all. But more importantly, he'd get to know this young lady a lot better than he did right now.

"Knew a feller from Misery," he said, his half smile broadening a bit. "Eva time you tell him sometin, he had two words for you."

"Oh? And what were they?"

"He say, 'Show me.'"

By the time Handy left, both he and Ella Mae had made a pact to take one another up on teaching him to speak better.

Walt, Marcus Easton's right-hand man, who hadn't done so good initially trying to take Ella Mae from Ferris House, reported to his boss down the street that night. He had just come from spying on Ella Mae through one of the front windows.

"Did you find out anything?" Easton asked him anxiously.

"Yeah, boss," Walt said, still having trouble speaking properly after his confrontation with Dallas Bodeen. "She spent some time talking to some big nigger, acting like she likes him by the time they were through."

"Likes him, eh? Well, I think it's time to teach that woman a lesson," Easton said in a spiteful voice filled with hate.

"What you got in mind, boss?"

"Simple. We'll see how she likes her friend wrapped in bandages."

"Yeah." A crooked smile came to Walt's face as he visioned in his mind just what his boss intended. Perhaps there was even a chance for some revenge on his own part. "Now you got the right idea, boss."

CHAPTER
★ 16 ★

Still got a bur under your saddle, do you, Wilson?" Carny Hadley sat across the noon campfire he and his brother had made, enjoying what he hoped would be a good cup of coffee. But Wilson still had that godawful look on his face, the way Carny remembered all of the Hadley boys looking when they had to take castor oil for what ailed them as children. (He never would admit to it, but some of the whiskey they'd drunk over the years had tasted just as bad or worse than any castor oil he'd ever taken.) The trouble was, Carny knew what the bur under his brother's saddle was, and he wasn't too anxious to bring the subject up. Hell, Ike had tried to make fun of it the day after it had happened, and Wilson had knocked him flat on his ass. And Ike was his brother!

"What's it to you, Carny?" Wilson growled at his

brother in what could only be a fighting mood. Wilson drove a fist into the palm of his hand. "I wish I had that son of a bitch right here, right now. I'd teach him a lesson he'd never forget."

"Sure you would, Wilson. Sure you would," Carny said in a voice that conveyed less than total confidence in his brother's fighting ability. On the other hand, Carny Hadley had seen Handy Partree once, and fought against him once, and once was enough on both counts. He had always thought that was the main difference between him and Wilson, his older brother. Wilson had always been a pure out-and-out grudge fighter, while Carny had the good sense to know when it was time to move on. And Wilson had never taken to being beaten, not by Chance Carston, not by anyone. He had found it particularly appalling to be beaten by a black man. Namely, this Handy Partree who had just drifted into town.

Carny dodged his brother when Wilson, fire in his eyes, tried to grab him by the shoulder and pull him near. Carny had never gotten used to his brother using him for a punching bag whenever he got mad or didn't get his way, especially when he was mad or drunk. Instead, he had learned to use his quickness, which, even for a man of his own bulky size, he could manage with certain parts of his body.

"I hope you git over that, Wilson," he said, largely ignoring his brother and his sour mood. "We didn't come out here to just sit and drink coffee and argue, you know."

Indeed they hadn't. Since they didn't really have a spread of their own, the Hadley brothers managed to make do by doing odd jobs about town or the area they lived in, counting on those they did the work for to provide them with enough reimbursement to be able to afford some of the necessities of life. Things like an occasional bottle of whiskey to wet your whistle with.

"Hello, the camp," a voice from out yonder said.

When the two brothers looked up, each saw more than half a dozen men riding toward them. Each of them also drew his six-gun in ready defense. This wouldn't be the first time that a party of men rode up to a campfire, feigning friendliness and wanting nothing more than your valuables by the time they had left. Not that the Hadleys had all that much to steal; they just didn't like someone making a bald-faced attempt with a six-gun to find out.

"That's close enough," Wilson said, still speaking in his half growl, half ugly voice, once the riders had come within fifty feet of their camp.

"That's right," Carny added, hefting his own six-gun, a revised Navy Model 1862 revolver. "I ain't potshot anyone all day." For emphasis, he gave the man a frown with his words. Unless you'd spent some time around the Hadley brothers, you wouldn't know that they put a lot of brag into what they could and couldn't do, mostly what they could do, since it was everyone else—they claimed—who talked about what they couldn't do.

"Now don't get hostile on us, friend," David Workman said in what he must have thought to be a jocular mood.

"Mister, as long as I got my brothers, I don't figure I need no friends, less'n my birthday comes about, and I usually head for the San Antonio red light district for that occasion," Carny said.

"You think this will easy your minds?" Abe Forrest said, and pulled back his cowhide vest to reveal a lawman's badge.

"It'd help an almighty lot," Wilson said, and holstered his six-gun, any fears he had, apparently put to rest. Then, to his brother, he said, "Go ahead, Carny, long as he's wearing a badge he should be all right. Hell, old man Carston ain't all that bad oncet you git to know him."

"Hope you ain't looking for coffee," Carny said as he put his Colt away. "I didn't make all that much to start with, but you're welcome to what's left."

A handful of the riders with Workman dug into their saddlebags and came up with cups, making their way to the fire and what remained of the coffeepot contents. When the pot was quickly emptied, Wilson Hadley said, "You boys make sure you clean that pot out now, you hear?" The three who shared the coffee silently nodded understanding.

"Now then, was you looking for us or just trying to scrounge up some extry of the black stuff for your riders?" Carny asked. Both he and Wilson had gotten to their feet as soon as Workman and his crew dismounted, still somewhat suspicious of them in the backs of their minds.

David Workman introduced himself and Abe Forrest and explained why they were this far south in Texas when they originally lived in Panhandle, all the way up north. He also explained—in a manner somewhat less truthful than Handy Partree or Chance Carston might have explained it—how badly they were wanting the black man for the murder of Ron Gentry in Panhandle. Workman did, however, mention how hard it would be to take Partree back to their town and how they had been nearly thrown out of town by the marshal and beaten by Handy Partree.

Wilson had a wide grin on his face at the word that this man had been beaten by Handy Partree. Carny knew all too well why it was there. He just hoped his brother didn't push the matter too much. The two of them taking on this bunch of yahoos would be nearly as bad as taking on Handy Partree again.

"That still don't tell me what in the devil you're doing out at my camp," Carny said when Workman was through speaking his piece.

David Workman's disposition went from one of a friendly stranger passing the time to one of pure business. A bit of a frown crossed his forehead as he looked at the Hadleys and said, "I did some asking around town and found out that you two men—if you are indeed Wilson and Carny Hadley—didn't fare too well against Partree either."

The smile was gone from Wilson's face, replaced by a dark red that crept up his neck, the pure embarrassment of the knowledge that he had lost a fight all too blatant to him now.

"I thought so," Workman said with a satisfied sneer.

"What's it to you?" Wilson asked in a growl.

Workman shrugged indifferently. "Nothing. I just thought you might like to make some money for a job I have in mind."

Carny frowned, already suspicious of what was being offered to him. "Money?"

"As a matter of fact, yes," Workman said. "And it involves Handy Partree."

Carny suddenly noticed that Abe Forrest, the lawman, was nowhere in sight. On giving the area a brief scan, he thought he saw the man tightening the cinch on his horse. It was almost as though he wanted nothing to do with the proceedings that were taking place between the Hadleys and Workman.

Or did he?

CHAPTER
★ 17 ★

Handy Partree's first day of work at Reed's Livery went quite well. He had reported for work bright and early to impress Harvey Reed, a medium-sized man who looked as though he could desperately use a man the size of Handy for the horseshoeing end of his livery business. Not that Harvey wasn't a capable man. He was fine as far as doing business and keeping the books straight, but he didn't have the size or bulk or strength needed to properly fit a horseshoe. Harvey knew that if you didn't fit a shoe the right way, why, you were likely to lose a customer, and any business-man would tell you that was bad commerce. To say he was relieved when Handy Partree showed up and offered to help him out would be understatement. Harvey was about to break out the bottle, and he wasn't a drinking man.

Once Handy had gotten a good solid fire going, and gotten used to the tools he had to deal with, it seemed just like the old days back on the plantation. He had learned a number of different trades back then, including that of a smithy and a carpenter. And he had kept his hand at both, for there was no telling when a man might be in need of either—or both. One thing Handy did know was that if the smithy job had fallen through, he was sure he would be able to find work doing a fair amount of carpentry around Twin Rifles. He could always start at the Carston spread, remembering that the horse corrals, especially the ones the Carston brothers used for breaking their wild mustangs, needed a good deal of repair. In the short time he had been there, he recalled that some of those mustangs acted meaner than any plantation foreman he had ever worked for. There had also been plenty of work that needed doing around town on various buildings he'd seen. Why, shoot, if this town was as old as that Mexican War, he ought to be able to rebuild it, and take his own good time doing it!

"Why don't you go get something to eat, Handy," Harvey Reed said, slapping the big man on the shoulder about noontime. "You've put in the better part of a day's work already," he added in a meaningful voice. If Harvey's calculations were right, Handy Partree had finished nearly a quarter of the work he had on back order just this morning. Once he'd put the word out that his new blacksmith would be starting work this morning, there had been an influx of visitors to town, including a good many farmers and ranchers in the area. Every one of them had been impressed with Handy's work, even when they discovered the color of his skin. One of them had even shaken Handy's hand, telling him he did good work.

Handy set his hammer and tongs aside and grabbed the folded cloth napkin he had brought to work with him this morning.

"Unless I'm mistaken, that's Margaret Ferris's ham and a couple of her biscuits you got there," Harvey said with a sniff of the nose and a smile, as Handy unfolded the napkin.

"You be right, Mr. Reed." There were several thick slices of ham Margaret and Rachel Ferris had served up on their breakfast menu, along with as many biscuits. He may not have been an able blacksmith, but Harvey Reed had a good nose.

He was also a curious man. After observing Handy for a minute in silence, Harvey said, "I suppose you're gonna eat down here because . . ." His voice trailed off, as though he hoped the black man would fill in the last portion of the sentence.

"Mr. Reed, I was brought up to stand in dah white man's shadow," Handy said in a hard tone. "It jes' git kinda hard with mah size and all. But I tries. Yes suh, I tries."

"I see. I didn't mean to pry."

Handy smiled to himself as he picked up the same tongs he'd used to hold the horseshoes he worked on, picked up a piece of ham with them, and stuck the meat over the nearby fire to warm it up. With a glance toward Harvey Reed, he said, "Always surprise me how folks apologize for what they already did."

Harvey's neck flushed a bright red. His grin was sheepish as he said, "Yes, I suppose you're right."

Handy ate his meal in relative silence, glancing every once in a while at Harvey Reed as Harvey tended to his chores around the livery stable. When he was through eating, he folded up the napkin and tucked it in his pocket. Returning it to Miss Margaret tonight would be his excuse for seeing Ella Mae again, he reasoned. Thinking about the pretty black woman and his growing attraction to her made Handy curious about the town they'd both recently come to.

"Tell me, Mr. Reed, how is it most of you folk is treating me so white?" he asked before going back to work.

"What do you mean?"

"Most of dah folk I met in dis town, they friendly toward me, you unnerstand? Why, I only been mouthed two, three times, and you ask me, they was strangers for sure."

"Well, Handy, I reckon you've just answered your own question," Harvey said with a grin. When Handy gave a confused frown, he continued. "This is a small town, and most of us know one another by our first names. Hell, the younger ones likely grew up with one another. Between the Mexican War, the War Between the States, and the Indians, why, I reckon we've all had occasion to help one another get through some tough times. Yes, we have. Near as I can figure, it's like having one big family, as well as we know each other. Oh, there's quarrels and spats now and again, but nothing worth shooting over."

"Den, how I answer mah own question?" Handy was still a bit confused.

"Well, it's those fellas that flannel-mouthed you, Handy. The Hadleys live a ways out of town, and I never did hear of that Workman and his crowd. They're strangers, see," he continued, "and I reckon if you was to ask anyone in Twin Rifles, they'd come right out and tell you that *strangers* is what causes most of our troubles."

Without another word Handy went back to his tongs and hammer, the discussion through as far as he was concerned. He didn't indicate one way or the other whether he understood—or cared about—the words Harvey Reed had spoken to him. He stayed that way the rest of the afternoon, the only noise he made being the sound of his hammer as he worked on horseshoes. By the time the evening meal came around, Harvey Reed had informed those of his customers who were still waiting for service that if they would return the next day, he would guarantee they would be taken care of.

Handy had finished over half of the backlog of work Harvey Reed had for him, with not one of the customers coming anywhere close to complaining about his work; in fact, most of them were well-pleased. Handy wondered whether they acted so astonished because of the quality of his work or because they were surprised a black man could actually do a good job.

When the last customer of the day was gone, Harvey thanked Handy again and was about to walk away when he turned back. "Why don't you call me Harvey?" he asked. "There ain't many men in this town that call me Mr. Reed."

The words shocked Handy. He had spent the entire day with this man and had come to the conclusion that he would be a fair man to work for. Not once had Harvey Reed cursed him or given him a dirty look or threatened to beat him if he didn't speed up. The fact of the matter was, Harvey Reed was a downright pleasant man. Still, Handy had his doubts. Or perhaps it was simply the fact that based on past experience, he didn't make friends with white men all that quickly.

"I'll think 'bout it, Mr. Reed," he said. "I figga dah time ready, I'll take you up on you offa."

CHAPTER
★ 18 ★

Taking the napkin back to Margaret Ferris served as a good excuse to see Ella Mae that evening, Handy thought. If anything, Margaret Ferris seemed to know what he was up to, for she merely thanked him for the return of the cloth napkin, gave him a rather warm smile, and said, "Ella Mae's in the kitchen with Rachel. Girl talk and all. But I'm sure she'd rather talk to you than to my daughter. Why don't you have a seat, Handy."

Without a word, Handy Partree took a seat at the community table closest to the kitchen. It was almost as though it was his place of honor, he thought, except for the fact that with this type of seating, honor seldom had much to do with it. Mostly it was to keep him away from the white customers.

"By the way, have you had supper yet?" Margaret asked halfway to the kitchen door. It was past the hour of the evening meal, the community tables now empty, and Handy thought it an odd question.

"Yes, ma'am," he replied with a smile. "Et over to the Porter's. Mighty fine chicken they serve."

With a polite smile, Margaret quietly disappeared into the kitchen, reappearing in only a few minutes with a steaming cup of coffee and a plate containing a fork and a huge slice of apple pie. Trailing her was a somewhat shy Ella Mae. When she plunked the plate and coffee cup down before Handy, she turned to Ella Mae, who was almost hiding behind her skirts, and said with the sternness of a mother speaking to her child, "Now, you sit down here and give this young man some conversation. Your workday is over, you know," she added, as though to inform the young lady that it was now all right to visit with Handy as much as she might like. Margaret took a few steps toward the kitchen, then stopped, as though something important had struck her, something that needed saying. "Sarah Ann makes fine fried chicken, but the day hasn't dawned when she could outdo my deep-dish apple pie," she said with a confident smile before disappearing into the kitchen.

That was how their evening had started, both of them acting a bit shy at the prospect of holding a lengthy conversation with one another. But after a few minutes of hesitant utterings, that was exactly what they did. For the most part they were still getting to know each other, but Ella Mae took the time to once again offer to help Handy learn the proper way of speaking in this white man's land. They spent an hour going over a number of the words Handy admitted to

145

making a mess of in his daily speech. At the end of an hour and a half, he found himself stretching and yawning.

"I bess git to the livery, Miss Ella Mae," he said, feeling suddenly tired from a hard day's work. "Mr. Reed, he fixed me up dah spare room in back of de stables."

Ella Mae, who had been quite outspoken in their time together and acted very much the teacher, now reverted back to the shy young lady who had first appeared from the kitchen not all that much earlier. "Too bad I've got a room upstairs," she said in a sheepish manner.

"Thank you lucky stars you got a room," Handy said in reply.

"No, silly." Ella Mae smiled in what Handy thought to be a foolish little girl way. "Then I could ask you to walk me home, don't you see?"

Neither one of them noticed Margaret Ferris come along then to pick up Handy's empty coffee cup. In the process, she managed to hear this much of their conversation. And, as anyone in Twin Rifles would admit to, she couldn't help but comment on what they were saying.

"Why don't you escort Ella Mae up to her room, Handy," she volunteered. "Show her what a gentleman you are."

"Ma'am?" He seemed somewhat confused at Margaret's words, but that didn't stop the older Ferris woman, who now was on a mission of sorts.

"But only to the door, you understand. A true gentleman never goes any farther than that unless he's invited in by the lady he's escorting."

As hard as Handy swallowed, you'd have thought

he'd just swallowed one of the many horseshoes he had worked on that day. He simply wasn't sure what he should do, and wound up following his mother's lessons on manners by mumbling "Yes, ma'am," and waiting for further instructions.

"Well, get to it, you two," Margaret said, before quickly disappearing from the scene.

"Come on, I'll show you where my room is," Ella Mae said, standing up and taking Handy's big fist in her own small palm as she led him toward the stairs.

Silently, they walked up the stairs, Handy taking in what appeared to be a vast amount of rooms. Ella Mae, on the other hand, felt a warmness within her that she had never experienced before. There was a certain comfort in having this big man next to her, having him hold her tiny hand in his own. It seemed odd at first, but by the time they reached her door, Ella Mae had gained an assurance that with this man beside her, she could never again be harmed by the likes of Marcus Easton. It was a gratification she had not felt in some time.

"Well, here it is," she said nervously, not even sure of the words she mumbled, she was that taken with Handy Partree's presence.

"Looks nice," he said when she slowly opened the door so he could see the interior of the room. "Lots betta than where I be sleeping."

In that instant, Ella Mae desperately wanted to tell Handy Partree about Marcus Easton and the trouble he was causing in her life. But it was only a passing desire, and she stopped herself before any of the words came out, knowing full well that the man before her must have his own problems to deal with.

"I betta go," Handy said, saving her from having to

147

explain the somewhat pained look on her face. "But I enjoy the lesson in my letters. You smart for a lady, I say that."

"Well, thank you, Handy," she replied with a smile. "That's the nicest compliment I've had in a long time." She took his hand in both of hers and shook it, the look on her face brightening considerably. "Will I see you tomorrow evening?"

"Yes, ma'am, I believe you will."

She watched the big man leave, following his movements all the way down the stairs and out the entrance door of Ferris House, a warm feeling building inside of her.

Handy could have sworn there was a certain spring in his step as he headed back toward the livery stable, although he wasn't about to admit that it was due to the last couple of hours he had spent with Ella Mae. He'd had too many letdowns in his life to be anything less than a cynic where the subject of romance was concerned. On the other hand, there was definitely something about that woman that made him feel drawn to her with the natural feelings a man will have for an attractive woman. And Ella Mae was indeed attractive in the eyes of Handy Partree. He told himself to forget it, but somehow he couldn't. He had her on his mind as he strolled back to the livery at the far end of town.

The sun had been down for nearly an hour now, but he found himself learning the ways of the people of this fair town. Even walking in near total darkness seemed easy to him, for he didn't bump into unfamiliar objects like some stranger might. With that in mind, it also made him wonder if he might have a place in Twin Rifles. Could he possibly fit in the community? Could he be more than just a proficient blacksmith in this territory? Without a doubt he had taken a job that was apparently much in need in Twin Rifles and the surrounding area, and everyone he had come in contact with in that trade was pleased with his work. So they couldn't consider him a shiftless, no-account drifter or loiterer, as might be the case elsewhere. No, there was simply the color of his skin that stood in the way of progress for Handy Partree. But then, it always would.

Ever since he could remember, he had been cautious of white people, especially the way in which they tried to trick and degrade the black folks around them. People like the Hadley brothers came to mind. They were bigots to be sure, the kind of men who cared for no one but themselves. And that particular memory brought up the question of whether it would ever be worth trying to establish himself in a town like Twin Rifles. After all, with as many decent people as he had come across so far, there were still the Hadleys of this world to contend with. It was another consideration to keep in mind when the time to make a final decision came. It was something he found weighing heavy on his mind as he approached the livery stable.

There were only two of them, but that must have been all they figured they needed to do in Handy Partree. He didn't notice the first one until he made some noise stepping out of the shadows of the livery doors, but by then it was too late. He brought the toe of a hard leather boot up into Handy's stomach, causing Handy to fold over from the force of the blow. His partner stepped up on Handy's other side and broke a heavy piece of deadwood over his back, leaving splinters of dried wood in the back of Handy's faded red work shirt. Then, when Handy was on his knees, he could have sworn the two of them were both beating on his neck and shoulders with the sharp end of the butt of each man's revolver. All he knew was, he hurt like hell and these fellows had the upper hand on him.

"What the hell!"

The words sounded familiar, as though he'd heard the voices before, but if they were from the men trying to beat him up, they sounded as though they had come from a distance.

He had to get his assailants off of him, and he had to do it soon. With one mighty thrust, he swung his arm up in between what he suspected was the middle of one assailant's legs. When his wrist hit something soft and he heard a painful scream fill the air, he knew he had struck one of them in his elsewheres. It was a hell of a way to get a man's attention, but an effective one to be sure.

It was then Handy Partree got the surprise of his life. Not only did the man he'd struck back off real quick like, but the other man, his partner in crime, suddenly did the same. And when Handy quickly got to his feet, he saw not two men, but four. And two of them were the Hadley brothers, the same ones he had thrown out of Ernie Johnson's saloon that first day he'd ridden into town! But if that wasn't surprise enough, the two Hadleys had taken to beating the devil out of the two men who had been attacking Handy.

For one long minute Handy Partree didn't know what in the world to do. He simply couldn't think worth a lick as he watched the two assailants all but crawl off into the darkness as the Hadley brothers, a satisfied look about them, wiped their hands together as though just getting rid of so much dirty garbage.

"Well, I be damned," Handy said in amazement.

"What you fellers pokin' you selves into my affairs for?"

Wilson Hadley, who was also at a loss for words, could do nothing but shrug and say, "It was dark and we couldn't make out who you were." The way he said it sounded as though he were trying, in his own clumsy way, to apologize for helping Handy Partree out.

"It was an honest mistake," Carny Hadley added. "It's just that me and Wilson always like a good fight. Must have forgot we was by the livery stable. Believe me, next time we see you in trouble like this, we'll make sure and see who it is we're getting involved with afore we start to swinging."

With that, the Hadley brothers made a hasty retreat from the area, only occasionally looking back at Handy Partree, who was standing there at the livery stable entrance, watching them go.

This was the first time in his life he could ever remember a bigot—or even a pair of bigots—helping him out at anything.

CHAPTER
★ 19 ★

The same night that Handy Partree nearly got the stuffing beat out of him, Chance Carston had a similar experience. It almost seemed as if fate had set the whole thing up, as though both men were doomed to suffer at the hands of attackers that night.

On one of the rare occasions that he didn't eat at Ferris House—for no matter how much he bragged about his bachelorhood, Chance Carston had a crush on Rachel Ferris, and seeing her at the boardinghouse over a meal was as close as he could get to her—Chance ate his evening meal with his brother at the Porter Cafe. Wash had wanted to talk to his brother about the number of mustangs they would be breaking in the not too distant future, and the promise of a free meal of Sarah Ann's fried chicken seemed about the only way to get Chance to sit in one place long enough to talk to him.

But they had spotted Handy at a table when they entered Big John's place and had taken a seat with him, the conversation turning to his first day at Reed's Livery and how he liked the work. It wasn't until Handy had finished his meal and excused himself to head over to Ella Mae at Ferris House that Chance and Wash got around to discussing mustangs and the pains of rounding them up and breaking them. Money seemed to be more on Wash's mind than his own, Chance noticed. Or was it the fact that his brother, now being a family man and all, was *worrying* more about the money they spent and didn't have? Whenever he saw Wash take on like this, Chance held firm in his resolve to remain a bachelor. At least, until the next time he saw Rachel.

It was well past an hour after sunset that Big John noticed the crowds were thinning out and told his daughter to take the rest of the night off. Sarah Ann gave her father a big hug, told him she loved him, and immediately headed for the door when the last customer was served.

"I want to tell you that this job doesn't get any easier, not at all," she said as she undid her shoes in the buckboard and took them off once they had reached the edge of town. "My feet are killing me." She made the statement with a good deal of anguish, obviously hoping Wash, seated next to her, his horse tied behind the buckboard, would give her feet a good rubbing once they were home. Chance had noticed in the last year and a half that Sarah Ann had gotten his brother trained real good, as far as tending to her went. Nor did Wash seem to mind.

Riding up next to his brother and sister-in-law, he could see Sarah Ann's dainty feet balanced on the buckboard, resting. Considering the fact that a man hardly saw a woman turn an ankle, much less an entire foot, Chance gulped hard at what he had just seen in the dim moonlight. But once he had his composure back, he was the same old Chance.

"Ah, young love," he said with a snicker when one of Sarah Ann's feet disappeared down by her husband's feet. "Ain't even home yet and she's playing footsie with him. Wouldn't you know."

"Oh hush, Chance, you're terrible," Sarah Ann said, only slightly perturbed. It wasn't the first time Chance had heard those words, or that tone of voice. In fact, he was almost certain that Sarah Ann, had she been in full light, would be shown to be blushing right now.

"At least I admit it, sis," he replied.

When they reached the ranch house, Wash made sure to pull the buckboard as close to the front of the house as possible, giving his wife that much less distance to travel to the front door. "You want to take care of the buckboard, Chance?" he asked his brother when he saw Sarah Ann limp slightly. Then, being chivalrous as any knight in shining armor he'd ever read about, Wash got off the buckboard, swept Sarah Ann up in his arms, and carried her into the house as though it were their wedding night.

"Oh thanks, sweetheart," Sarah Ann said when she got through kissing Wash inside. "I really appreciate it."

Outside, Chance led the lone mare over to the barn and undid the rigging on her, pushing the buckboard over by the corral. He had it in mind to give old Dolly a good rubdown and feeding. She likely deserved it, considering that once she hauled Sarah Ann into the Porter Cafe each morning, she did nothing but sit in the shade of the side alley until Sarah Ann returned at night. God help the horse if the sun overshone that part of the alley for any extended period of time. She'd likely break free of her reins and run clear to the Rio Grande.

With Handy there had been two assailants, but with Chance there were three. They came out of nowhere while he was rubbing down Dolly, meaning they came out of the shadows of the barn door, not unlike Handy's assailants. The first one came up behind Chance and surprised him with a hard punch to the side, which not only doubled Chance over, but made Dolly rear, whinny, and run out of the ranch yard.

When the horse was gone, the second assailant came at Chance from what would have been the far side of the horse he'd been rubbing down. Chance had gone to one knee. When the man tried to kick him in the head, he was quick enough to move to the side, the assailant kicking him in the shoulder instead. The kick hurt like hell, but Chance Carston was a fighter, if anything, and made a point of grabbing the man's boot with one big hand, twisting it to the side and knocking him off balance so he fell over on his side.

"Chance! What's going on out there!" Wash yelled from the front porch, having heard the mare run off.

"Company!" Chance yelled, knowing his brother would hear the urgency in his voice. In their days as Texas Rangers, the two brothers had worked out a code of their own, a single word that let the other one know trouble was near or about. That one word seemed to fit their needs, and, over the years, when one brother would yell it out, he could be sure the other was on his way.

155

Wash was indeed on his way to his brother's aid, but he had taken off his gun belt and his boots, so he could only hope that joining in fisticuffs would be enough as he ran toward the barn.

The first man kicked Chance in the side while the third man, who had apparently been hesitant to join in the melee, came out of the shadows with a knife in hand. He lashed out at Chance as the older Carston went down from the kick, cutting him on the arm and bloodying his sleeve.

Wash made a diving tackle at the kicker, knocking him to the ground and grappling with him until he was on top of him and hitting him as hard as he could.

Bloody as he was, Chance managed to reach for his side and the bowie knife he carried as a constant companion, ready to take on the knife wielder or the second man, who was now on his feet. It wasn't the first time he had faced two-to-one odds, for there had been worse days in his life. But getting out of those fixes had proven to be tough going, and even in his own front yard, Chance was finding out that blood was still red and fear was still fear. And now he had two of these bastards to take care of and he was the wounded man.

He didn't have to.

A gunshot filled the night air, and as soon as it went off, so did the assailants. Like most bullies, they fought hard when the odds were in their favor, but at the first sign of serious injury to themselves, took off like a pack of scared jackrabbits.

The knifer grabbed his friend, who had managed to throw Wash off of him once the gunshot went off—more out of pure terror than any kind of strength, Chance was sure—and helped him from the scene, fading into the night as quickly as they had appeared.

The third man had cut and run at the first sign of gunfire.

In a moment Chance was on his feet, his Colt's Conversion Model .44 in hand, looking for something to shoot at. Out of the corner of his eye he confirmed his suspicions. Sarah Ann stood on the porch, one of his Colt's Army Model .44's in her hand, ready to fire it a second time if the need arose, he was sure. Rather than try and hit one of the intruders, she had wisely shot into the air, an act that had scared them as effectively as if she had tried to potshoot them. But with her own husband and Chance mixed among them, she wasn't about to try any heroics. For one instant Chance found himself grateful that his sister-in-law was a level-headed woman.

He didn't put the six-gun away until he heard the sound of hooves galloping off into the distance.

"My God, Chance, you're hurt!" Sarah Ann said when he approached the house, nearly all of his left arm a bloody red color.

Wash had run into the house, yanked on his boots and gun belt, and was now pulling the reins from the back of the buckboard, mounting his own horse.

"I'm going to get Dolly," he yelled from his horse before kicking its sides and leaving.

"What about them?" Sarah Ann asked, not even knowing who they were but having to call them something.

"Ain't enough moon out to track 'em, sis," Chance said as he made his way into the house. A man never gets used to the sight of his own blood, and Chance Carston was no exception as he plunked himself down on a wooden chair, feeling a bit faint.

Sarah Ann seemed to suddenly be in a frenzy, running about and gathering up water and cleaning material for his wound. It wasn't until she had them all on the kitchen table that she stopped for a moment, gathered up a lungful of breath, and asked, "But who were they? And what did they want?"

Chance, who was also out of breath, even though he didn't feel as though he'd accomplished much, looked at Sarah Ann, slowly shook his head and said, "Beats the hell outta me, sis. Beats the hell outta me."

CHAPTER
★ 20 ★

To David Workman, the War Between the States had always been a useless conflict. Who cared what the people in Washington, D.C.—much less the politicians!—had to say about slavery and the fate of the Negro in this country? Certainly, he didn't. But the closer the abolitionists got to him, especially when John Brown and his bunch moved into Kansas and that whole "Bleeding Kansas" thing erupted in the 1850s, the more he was forced to look at the possibility of one day losing his slaves. And he had too many good ones to lose without putting up a fight. So he prepared for the worst, hiring men who were as good with their guns as they were at working cattle or any other dumb animals he might have. When the war did start, he had these men patrolling the borders of his land, maintaining a well-armed force that could fight off any Union or Confederate army unit that trespassed on his property. By God, no one was going to push David Workman around, no one!

Fortunately, the war had mostly stayed away from the state of Texas, only one or two minor skirmishes taking place in the four-year-long duration. That suited David Workman just fine, for he had enough troubles of his own during the war years. Market sales were down—hell, there *wasn't* any market—and the Indians in the territory had acted up something fierce once the few army posts in the area were nearly deserted—all but a handful of forces had been pulled back East to fight the war. That left every man to defend what was his own, and that had turned out to be a real chore. No, sir, the war years had been no fun, even if you weren't fighting alongside the Johnny Rebs or Billy Yanks.

It was when the war had ended that David Workman found himself in real trouble. Not only had Lincoln freed the slaves, but that damned Freedmen's Bureau had come along, making themselves noticed anywhere the blacks might have had work as slaves. They made sure the coloreds were informed that they were free and could work for wages now, instead of doing what they had been forced to do for years for no pay. The trouble for David Workman had been—even if he didn't want to admit it to himself—that nearly all his former slaves had decided to find work elsewhere rather than stay and work for a man they considered a slave driver. That included Handy Partree, who had been one of his better workers. In fact, Handy had been one of the few who had even stayed in the region, moving just down the road to Henry Morrison's outfit once the rancher had returned from the war. And from what Workman had heard over the years, Morrison had turned a run-down operation into a real working ranch a man could be proud of owning.

Not to David Workman's surprise, Morrison had high praise for Handy Partree as a working hand. At first Workman had let the compliments about Handy go, but as the years passed—three years of high praise, no less—Morrison had more and more to say about Handy that was praiseworthy, especially around Workman. And, being the jealous and arrogant man that he was, Workman found himself taking a great deal of offense at the fact that Morrison was making as much money out of Handy Partree's work in those three short years as he had made in more than ten years of owning the Negro. How dare Morrison make more money at something than he had! It soon became clear to those who worked around David Workman that the man could easily become crazy mad at the slightest mention of Handy Partree or Henry Morrison, so it was generally agreed among the Workman crew that these particular individuals' names would not be mentioned in the presence of their boss.

Obsessed as he was with this hatred, it wasn't until Ron Gentry had gotten killed that David Workman decided that it had all been a ruse of Morrison's, to make him lose control of himself and his ranch. But now, with Morrison dead, Workman figured he could get Handy Partree back.

Hearing the casual comments of the old general-store owner, a germ of an idea spread in Workman's mind and grew into a full-blown devious conspiracy. As powerful as he was, he convinced the store owner to close his general store for an hour, and led him by the elbow over to Marshal Abe Forrest's office. On the way there he told the man exactly what he would tell the marshal, whether it was true or not. Thus was invented the story he had been telling everyone who would listen, since the marshal, Workman, and his men had left Panhandle.

What he didn't tell anyone, not even Abe Forrest, was that one way or another, he planned on seeing Handy Partree die before his trek was done. There was no way he could let a man like Partree live, not after making a fool out of him the way he had, with the help of Henry Morrison, of course.

The fact of the matter was, *Handy Partree had to die!*

That was why Workman had hired those big brutes he had met outside of Twin Rifles. At first he would see if they were any good at following orders, and he offered to pay them fifty dollars each—an advance of one double eagle to each of them—if they could beat the living hell out of Handy Partree. He figured it would take the two of them, big as Handy was. If they could do that, he would see what they thought about killing Partree for a hundred dollars. But they hadn't done that, not at all. Now, at the creek he and his men were camped at outside of Twin Rifles, David Workman was listening to them give some feeble excuse about breaking up a fight that was already in progress when they got to the livery stable.

"What do you mean you couldn't beat him up!" he yelled at them, his face red with hatred. "What were you, afraid you'd have to split that pittance I gave you with the two culprits who got there before you? You greedy bastards!"

He had a whole mouthful more he wanted to say but never did, for Wilson Hadley had a fistful of his shirt and had pulled it over to him, the look on his face as mean as the flannel-mouth felt. "Don't ever call me that again, Workman," he growled. "I know who my daddy was."

The two gunmen in Workman's crew who kept trying to prove they were good with the weapons at their side—Derth and Shannon, by name—went for their revolvers, but their hands stopped on the butts of their six-guns. What kept them from pulling their guns out any farther was the deadly look on Carny Hadley's face. It was a look that said they would wind up in a shallow grave if they made another false move, and neither one of them wanted to die this young.

Wilson Hadley pushed David Workman away, making the man stumble backward and almost lose his balance. "Don't you worry, Workman," he said, still growling like a mad puma that has just been disturbed, "me and Carny don't make no promises we can't keep. You'll git your money's worth, you just wait and see. Hell, I can't help it if that big black sonofabitch has got more enemies in town than either of us do. You'll git your money's worth."

Then, abruptly, the two of them turned to leave. Having loosened the cinches on their mounts, they had left them at the creek to drink their fill. They stood there, letting their horses drink in their own good time before tightening the cinches.

Just as soon as Workman was through conversing with the Hadley brothers, another of his men rode into camp, three strangers with him. One of them was a tall man, well-dressed in a black frock coat. The two men with him could have been hired hands on anyone's ranch, from the look of them.

"Boss, I think you need to talk to this here fella," Workman's man said once they had dismounted. He

163

went on to introduce the man as Marcus Easton, the two men with him his hired hands.

"I understand we have something in common, Mr. Workman," Easton said in a superior tone of voice. Workman decided just from hearing it that he didn't really care for the man but that he'd listen to him.

"And what's that?"

Easton explained that it was his two men who had been sent down to the livery the night before to pay Handy Partree a visit and rough him up. "Those two men broke it up," he said, nodding in the direction of the Hadley brothers, who were still cinching up their mounts. He let Workman know he didn't appreciate it. When David Workman only grunted in a vulgar manner, Easton let the subject drop and went on to explain his reason for having Handy Partree beaten—that Handy apparently had eyes for the woman who was a maid at Ferris House, a Negro by the name of Ella Mae.

"She's mine," he said forcefully. "Or maybe I should say she *was* mine until the end of the war. A month ago she fled my plantation, running away. I tracked her down to this little borough. I intend to get her back, one way or another. If this Handy, or whatever his name is, is indeed her beau, I intend to teach him a lesson. And perhaps Ella Mae too, if you get my drift."

"I know what you mean," Workman said, his voice still a grumble. "And that's what you figure we got in common, these two niggers who are acting like girl and boy lovers?"

"That's right," Easton said, producing a long, thin cigar from inside his coat pocket. He bent down, picked up a small piece of deadwood that had caught fire, and applied it to the end of his cigar, drawing in a few puffs. "It occurs to me that we might join forces, having basically the same objectives in mind."

Along with everything else he was, David Workman was also a grudge fighter. It was useless to bear a grudge against the dead, so Henry Morrison was no longer in need of his hate. Derth and Shannon and one of the other men had apparently made an impression on that Carston character, cutting him up good from what they had said. (He had hated that Carston fellow ever since that run-in at the sutler's store up in Fort Griffin; besides, the man had a hard fist.) Maybe being cut like he was would make the man think twice before butting into his affairs. That left Handy Partree on his list, and he wanted Handy in the worst way now. Still, it took him a while before he looked up at Marcus Easton, somewhat cautiously.

"All right, maybe we can lend each other a hand with this mess," he said in an even tone. "But when it's over, we go our separate ways."

"Agreed," Easton said jubilantly, and stuck out his hand. "We should wrap this up in no time."

If David Workman seemed a bit hesitant when he stuck out his own paw, it was because he desperately wanted to count his fingers when Easton released his grip, just to make sure he still had all of them. To say he trusted the man would be folly.

"You say Handy is shining up to this girl, is that right? Ella Mae?" Workman said in thought.

"That's a fact." Marcus Easton raised a curious eyebrow to David Workman. "Got something in particular in mind?"

"Now that you mention it, yeah," Workman said, slowly nodding.

"Well, speak up, man, speak up."

"Let me ask you something, Easton. It ever cross

your mind that with this nigra girl *in* the picture, maybe the best thing to do is take her *out of it?*"

Easton's face brightened. "I see what you mean."

Figuring that out hadn't been hard at all, Workman thought to himself. In fact, it made him feel much better. With a partial smile, he said, "Easton, why don't you and your boys light and set and have you some coffee."

As he poured their coffee, he gave a sideward glance at the creek. The Hadley brothers were nowhere to be seen.

CHAPTER
★ 21 ★

Despite what David Workman might have thought, Chance Carston had no intention of backing off or ignoring what had happened to him the night before. As far as he was concerned, you didn't dare let a man push you around or try to intimidate you. No, sir. Why, if you did that, the fellow would spend the rest of his life—or yours—walking all over you, until you couldn't put up with it anymore and left the town—or territory or state, take your pick. Chance had learned long ago that to let a man get the best of you was the wrong thing to do. Pa had always said that the best thing to do was meet the man head-on and get it over with. And that was just what Chance had in mind. The trouble was, he first had to find out who in the devil those three were who had taken after him last night. Pa had also told him years ago, when he'd first started with the Texas Rangers, that there was a lot to be said for not making false accusations to a man. A body could get killed doing such a thing, and that wasn't anywhere near healthful. Not at all.

Chance got his first clue as to what might be going on when he went into Adam Riley's office the next morning. Riley was slightly younger than Chance, and he'd moved to Twin Rifles a few years back and taken up residence as the local doctor. He was pretty good at what he did. Tall and good-looking, Riley had a reputation as having a good bedside manner with his patients, although Chance was sure there were more than a couple of the women in the territory who were wanting the man to perform more than simple manners at their bedside. If nothing else, Chance was sure he'd get his wound properly attended to at Adam Riley's.

"Now, what in the devil happened to you?" the doctor asked when Chance made his way into his office that morning. "I don't recall you Carstons having any longhorns to get gored by out at your spread. Or would that be a new addition for you?"

"No," Chance said with a smile, "I'm afraid it's nothing to do with goring steers, Doc. Run into a fella last night who was wielding an Arkansas toothpick and had designs on taking a chunk out of me with it. Fact is, him and his friends weren't none too friendly at all."

Adam Riley frowned as he began to undo Chance's makeshift bandage.

Sarah Ann had spent enough time bandaging her father over the years to be able to do a better than average job of taking care of Chance and Wash when the occasions arose, and last night was one of those occasions. She had thrown Chance's bloody work shirt over in the corner, reminding herself to save it for later, when she might be able to use it to mend bits and pieces of her husband's and brother-in-law's worn-out shirts. That morning she had a shirt ready for Chance to wear, the left sleeve already rolled up past the elbow. She had even helped him put it on as he gingerly slipped his rebandaged left arm through the shirtsleeve.

"There seems to be a lot of that going around," Riley said as he slowly removed the bandage from his patient's arm.

"Oh?" If Chance had appeared nonchalant about his wound when he first walked in—after all, the upper part of his body seemed to be nothing but scars from bullet and knife wounds—he was suddenly showing more than a little interest in the good doctor's comment. "How's that?"

"Well, there wasn't any knife or bullet wound to him, but your friend Handy paid me a visit late last night," Adam said, still busy working with the bandage. "It seems he was attacked by a couple of men too."

Chance was taken aback at the man's words. "Someone tried beating up Handy? From the way he's held his own hereabouts, I'd think whoever was trying it would have wanted a good half-dozen men to do it."

Adam Riley chuckled, to himself perhaps, if to no one else. "Yes, he is a pretty big man."

"How'd he fare?"

The doctor shrugged. "It could be worse. I told him he could very well have a fractured rib and that he should take it easy for a day or two." Riley was now inspecting the wound on Chance's arm, dabbing at it

169

with a sterile cloth Chance could only recognize as smelling of medicinal liquid. He was silent for a moment as he did this, then said, "It's a shame, you know."

Chance frowned, confused. "How's that?"

"I can't seem to get anyone in this town to listen to my advice unless it's a pregnant woman."

"I don't understand."

Riley half smiled, and nodded in the direction of a half-opened window. "Can't you hear?"

The doctor's office was only half a block away and across the street from Reed's Livery. Chance cocked an ear and, in what seemed like otherwise total silence, heard the echoing ping of a hammer, obviously that of Handy shaping or reshaping a horseshoe.

"Oh," he said, now aware of what the doctor was speaking about.

"Yes. I told him to take it easy, but there he is, hard at work with that hammer of his." The doctor now held an empty pan under Chance's arm as he gently poured what looked and smelled like alcohol over the wound, likely flushing it of any germs that might still be present. Chance could only grit his teeth, the way any man would who had gotten used to the type of wounds he had experienced in his lifetime.

"Can't blame him, in a way," Chance said when the doctor wiped his arm off and applied salve to the wound, beginning to dress it again. "He claimed last night that old Harvey Reed told all the rest of the day's customers to show up this morning and they'd have their work taken care of sure as rain."

"I don't know if putting up with that much pain is conducive with trying to make a good impression," Riley said with a raised eyebrow. "He might make a good impression on those folks, but he might be putting himself in bed for a while too, if he's not careful."

"I'll pass that on to him when I see him."

"I already have," Riley said, as though to tell Chance not to worry about making the wasted effort. "He did seem a bit chagrined when he left, though."

"Oh?" Chance found himself taking a particular interest in Doc Riley's story, the more it unfolded. "I wonder what caused that?"

"I don't know," the doctor said as he finished bandaging the arm. "Mumbled something about not being able to believe who it was who had broken the fight up. Or something to that effect."

Chance dug a dollar out of his pocket and laid it on the doctor's desk. "That oughta cover it."

Not long after returning from the war, Chance Carston had had occasion to visit the new doctor of Twin Rifles concerning a minor wound he had received. When he had dug out a dollar in payment, the doctor had reminded him that the bill was only two bits. It was then Chance had explained to the doctor that he had just deposited some money in the bank and could afford the one-dollar fee. Ever since, Chance and the doctor had a silent agreement that when he laid down a dollar—or whatever other sum of money might wind up on Doc Riley's desk—the good doctor could subtract two bits for Chance's visit and apply the remainder of the amount to anyone in the community who might be in arrears in owing him money, particularly those who couldn't really afford to pay him at this time. Neither Chance nor the doctor had ever breathed a word of this arrangement to anyone else, and Chance had considered it his own little way of repaying the community for any past favors. And he seemed to remember an awful lot of them, as he had grown up in Twin Rifles.

"Thanks," Riley said as Chance left his office, no other words being necessary between them.

Chance found what had happened to Handy to be just as interesting as Doc Riley's story about it, and headed straight for the livery when he left the physician's office. Sure enough, there was Handy, pounding away as hard as could be at another horseshoe.

"Doc says you might be doing yourself harm," he said to the big man, who all but ignored him until he'd finished fashioning the horseshoe into the size he wanted. It was only then that he looked up and gave an easy smile to Chance.

"Mr. Reed, he a nice man for de most part," he said, glancing at Harvey Reed, who now stood over in the shade of the livery, idly talking to one of the customers. "But he a businessman too, and de businessman in him, he want his money worth. You know?"

Chance returned the smile. "I know."

"Look like you been to trouble too," Handy said, taking in Chance's arm.

"Both of us, I reckon." Even at this early hour, Handy had taken his shirt off, and who could blame him, being this close to a fire. He made no exhibit of his bandaged midsection, nor did he try to hide it. To Handy, it was simply something that had happened, something he would live with, and that was that. "Mind me asking how you come on yours?" Chance asked, indicating the bandages about his chest.

"Eff you tell me you story."

Chance smiled again. "Sounds like an even trade."

In bits and pieces, Handy told Chance what had

happened to him, as Handy nailed the newly-formed horseshoe on a waiting mare's hoof. Chance decided that Doc Riley had gotten his story right, for what he heard from Handy sounded basically the same as what the town doctor had told him.

"Doc said you was acting kind of strange when you left his office," Chance said, hoping his words would egg the man on to a more complete and detailed story of what was going on in his mind.

"Oh, that," Handy said with a forced chuckle that made Chance believe he was actually a bit embarrassed about the whole thing.

"Yeah, that."

"Strange thing 'bout all of it, I din' know the fellers what attacked me, but these other two what busted up the fight—" Here he stopped and simply shook his head in disbelief.

"Yeah?" For an instant Chance was excited about what the answer would be.

"It were dem big brothers, de ones look ugly an act mean, you know?"

"The Hadleys?" Any excitement Chance might have felt was now nothing more than total astonishment. "The troublemakers?"

"Yeah, dat's dem." Handy went on to explain how the two had broken the fight up and then proceeded to give him some kind of strange excuse about why they did it after his attackers got away.

"Don't sound like the Hadley brothers at all," Chance said, not sure how to take this part of Handy's story. As much as they had mouthed off to Handy— or so Chance had heard—and as much as they supposedly hated Handy Partree and his color, why in the devil would they come to his aid? It simply didn't make any sense, none at all.

173

"Don' make no sense to me neither," Handy said when he saw the confused look on Chance's face.

"I know."

Handy made his way back to the fire, picked up another horseshoe with his tongs, and threw it in the fire to heat up. Then he looked back at Chance, a more serious look about him now.

"I tell you one thing, Chance," he said in a hard, even tone of voice.

"What's that?"

"One way or t'other, that Workman feller, he got him a hand in it." Handy gave Chance a wink and a nod to assure him of his words. "Now den, how you come by you injury?"

Chance told him what had happened to him, and by the time he was through, he was convinced that Handy Partree was right.

David Workman definitely had something to do with all of this.

CHAPTER

★ 22 ★

"You thinking the same thing I am?" Carny asked his brother Wilson. There was a worried tone to his hard voice, something that didn't often happen to Carny Hadley. But he had something difficult on his mind, and he could tell by the look on Wilson's face that his brother was worried almost as badly as he was.

"Yeah," the oldest Hadley growled in what he considered a normal tone of voice. "Something just don't figure here, and I'm having me a devil of a time ciphering it out."

Carny nodded in agreement. "Know what you mean. You get through puzzling on it, you let me know, 'cause I'm damned if I know."

Neither one of them had to say what was bothering them. The whole mess they had gotten themselves into concerning Handy Partree and David Workman was getting too confusing and too complicated to understand, much less believe.

That first run-in with Handy Partree hadn't really been anything out of the normal, for neither Wilson nor Carny had ever cared much for colored people.

But what had happened since then, why, it was enough to befuddle a body for eternity. First there had been that damn-fool agreement the two of them had made with that loudmouth Workman. Not that they couldn't use a hundred dollars apiece; hell, in today's economy, any man in this country could use a hundred dollars, even the big-time politicos, and they were the ones committing graft right out in the open. The strange thing was, when they tried and ambush Handy in the dark last night, they'd come on two other men who had gotten there before them. It was almost as if their instinct had taken over and they had set upon the men, throwing them off Handy Partree as though he were their nearest and dearest friend. And God help them if that should ever happen.

They had found out how truly offensive and loud-mouthed David Workman could be this morning when they decided to be honest with the man and explain what had happened to their own plan of action last night. They had planned on giving it another try tonight, but after seeing what kind of a jackass Workman could be, they were both having second thoughts. Still, it wasn't the second thoughts that had convinced them the man was not only a flannel-mouth, but underhanded as well, so much as what they had overheard at Workman's camp as they had cinched their horses and readied to ride.

It was that stranger and his compadres who rode into camp with one of Workman's crew that got them to worrying. True, they hadn't heard all of the conversation the two men had, but they had heard enough to make them wonder whether they were doing the right thing in getting involved with any kind of action against Handy Partree. Workman wanted to string him up for some killing he was supposed to have been involved with up north. Then this Easton—or was it Eastman?—wanted to get that new maid at Ferris House and pack her on back home—wherever that was—just like she was his own. And who was to say, maybe she was, even in this day and age. Some of them black folks still worked for the same masters as when they'd been slaves, you know. What was really bothering them, Wilson figured, was those last words they had heard Workman speak as they left his camp. Something about taking the Negro girl out of the picture. It was enough to rub a man raw, Wilson decided, and he didn't like it, not one bit.

"Saddle up, Carny," he finally said, having made his decision. "We're taking a ride."

"Where the hell we going?" Carny asked as he sloshed on his hat.

"To the Ferris House?"

"The Ferris House?" Carny was purely fluster. "What's there?"

Wilson gave his younger brother a sly smile. Digging in his pocket he produced a silver dollar, held it up for Carny to see. "I figured maybe I'd get us a supper meal . . . and the answers to some questions that are bothering me."

"My word, I haven't seen you boys in quite some time," a surprised Margaret Ferris said when Wilson and Carny made their way into her foyer.

Wilson grabbed the hat off his head, poking his brother in the ribs when Carny didn't immediately follow his lead. All the time he was moving, there seemed to be a thoughtful look about him. "Seven months, I'd say. Maybe eight, ma'am," he said in an apologetic tone. "You'll have to forgive me, ma'am, I disremember exactly."

Perhaps Wilson Hadley couldn't remember exactly, but Margaret surely did. It had been Thanksgiving day of last year that Pardee Taylor had brought Wilson and Carny Hadley to the church service, surprising not only Margaret, but the entire town, or at least those who had made an attempt to attend the services. But as Will liked to put it, that was a whole 'nother canyon. It was just one she wouldn't soon forget.

"Closer to eight months, I'd say." Margaret smiled in an honest effort to be cordial to these two town ruffians. "What can I do for you?"

Wilson glanced around the dining area, noticing that most of the customers had apparently already eaten and left. At first a look of worry crossed his face, soon replaced by a calmer, more controlled appearance. "We ain't too late for supper, are we?" he asked, a note of concern in his voice. In one quick motion, as though the world depended on it, he dug his lone silver dollar from his pocket, brandishing it for Margaret in particular as he held it out for her examination. "Got a dollar betwixt us, so I can pay for both meals. Yes, ma'am."

"Yes, boys, I'm sure we can rustle up something for you," she said in her politest manner, meaning every word of it.

"Oh, don't go out of your way, ma'am. Me and Carny, we'll eat just about anything you Ferris ladies can prepare," Wilson said, his face suddenly going red with embarrassment. He'd wanted to tell her that he knew how hard it was for these two women to fix the numerous meals they did, for he and his brothers had seen the very same thing done by their mother day in and day out for all of the Hadley boys when they were younger, and Ma was still alive. In fact, if you had caught Wilson in the right mood, he might even confide in you that he personally thought his mother had worked herself to death, waiting on her boys like she did. But Wilson wasn't too good at words, and as soon as he'd have spoken, he'd have known he could have said it better.

Margaret began to leave, then stopped and faced Wilson Hadley again. With a touch of mischievousness to her smile, she said, "Tell me, Wilson, just what food of mine is it that you *won't* eat?"

Certain he was about to get thrown out, Wilson summoned up the courage within him, gulped hard, and said, "Greens, ma'am. Never did care for greens." When Margaret's grin widened, he added, "That don't offend you, Miss Margaret?"

"No, Mr. Hadley, it doesn't offend me. You're entitled to your likes and dislikes." Then she disappeared into the kitchen, returning only to pour two cups of coffee for them. In a little more than five minutes she was back with their food, which consisted of three plates for each of them. The largest plate set before them contained several thick, steaming slices of roast beef. The two additional plates contained piles of fresh-made biscuits and home-fried potatoes. Margaret Ferris had no doubt that the Hadleys would have little trouble cleaning their plates, just like the Carston men she served, or any other man in town who had an admiration for hot food.

After setting the plates down, she refilled their coffee cups. As she did so, Dallas Bodeen walked by, the last of her evening customers to finish his meal. As he passed the Hadleys, she noticed that he gave them a harsh, disapproving look. A lot of people in town still found it hard to get used to the Hadleys and their sometimes strange ways. Dallas Bodeen was one of them.

When she filled their coffee cups a third time, she noticed they were nearly finished with their meal.

"Miss Margaret," Wilson said around a mouthful of food.

"Yes, Mr. Hadley." Still kind and considerate, that was Margaret. "What can I do for you?"

"What my brother wants to know, ma'am, is have you got time to sit and chew the fat a mite?" Carny said, swallowing his food before his brother could clear his mouth to speak.

"Yes, ma'am, that's it."

The look on Margaret's face was one of surprise, for being asked to sit and chew the fat was about the last thing she had ever expected to hear from the Hadleys. "Well . . . yes, I suppose so," she said in a cautious tone. The waitress in her wanted to be obliging to her customers, but there was something in the back of her mind that told her to be careful around these two. Or was it the echo of some of Will Carston's words of wisdom? Will could usually tell the good from the bad at first glance. But then, you expected that from the town lawman. "There's not that much left to cleaning up the dishes, and Rachel and Ella Mae seemed to be having a nice chat while they were at it, so I suppose I could spare a few minutes."

"Thank you, ma'am," Wilson said with a sigh of relief. "You don't know how hard it was for me to ask you . . ." He let the words trail off, not sure of how he should finish the sentence, or whether he should have started it to begin with.

"I got that impression, gentlemen," Margaret said, placing her coffeepot on the community table and taking a seat across from the Hadleys, who now had nothing more than coffee cups before them. When neither of the brothers sitting across from her said anything, she added, "Well, I'm listening, boys. Tell me a story."

Which is just what they did. And along with it, they told her everything that had been bothering them, from the run-in with Handy Partree to David Workman's words about something disastrous happening to Ella Mae. When they were through, both of the Hadleys seemed to be filled with a great deal of solace, as though the weight of the world had been lifted from their shoulders. If anyone had a look of concern about them, it was definitely Margaret Ferris. It wasn't so much for the dilemma the Hadleys had found themselves in, so much as it was for the jeopardy Ella Mae might be coming into in the near future.

"I'm glad you boys decided to have this conversation," she said. Now that she knew the possibility of something dangerous happening, Margaret Ferris felt a good deal more in control of the situation. Like Will Carston, she had never been big on surprises. "But tell me something. Why didn't you go to the marshal about this? Why come to me?"

Wilson chuckled to himself. "Ma'am, all we got to do is get within shouting distance of Will Carston and he'll be shoving the law down our throat and running us out of town. And that's a fact."

"He's right, Miss Margaret," Carny confirmed. "Besides, you're one of the few people who actually treats us decent. Figured we had us a better chance at palavering with you than your friend Will."

181

Margaret was flattered. "I think you boys deserve some pie," she said with a smile, and was gone, quickly returning with plates of good-sized portions of her deep-dish apple pie.

At any other time, these two might have done their best to devour the dessert as quickly as they could, but tonight they had certain things on their minds—the unanswered questions that seemed to plague Wilson —and decided they had to get this woman's advice while they had her in their grasp. Wilson stuffed one big forkful of pie in his mouth before looking at Margaret, who had taken her seat again, and studying her face.

"If you don't mind me asking, ma'am, what in the devil is it that's making a body feel so obfusticated about this whole situation?" Wilson asked. From the sound of his voice, she was sure he meant every word he spoke. In fact, she couldn't remember either of the Hadleys ever being as serious as they had been this past half hour they had been talking to her.

She knew that the obvious answer was that they were experiencing normal reactions to what on this frontier was a normal situation, considering that most men faced danger more often in Texas than they would if they had lived back East. At first Wilson's questions puzzled her, but then she realized that there wasn't an awful lot that was anything close to normal about these Hadleys. They had been brought up to be fighters from the first get-go, and were looked down upon by most as nothing more than bullies, trouble-makers, and drunks when they came to town. Because of that, few people in Twin Rifles would likely give them a first chance, much less a second chance. And Carny was probably right, if they had gone to Will to explain their situation, the first thing he would have done was pull his gun and ask them what kind of trouble they were in this time. It was time, Margaret decided, that someone gave these boys a chance to prove themselves.

"Well, Wilson, I think what happened was you experienced a genuine emotion," she said in a serious tone.

"Ma'am?" Wilson and Carny frowned at her.

"Don't you see, you're so used to fear and fighting that they are just about the only two things you know."

"What else is there?" Carny asked.

"Lots of things, Carny," she said, placing a gentle hand on his big paw. "I think what you've just experienced is *compassion*. You started caring about someone besides yourselves. And that someone was Handy Partree."

Both Wilson's and Carny's eyes almost bugged out in amazement at the words they were hearing. "But it can't be him!" Wilson said in a louder than usual tone. "Why, he's a—"

"He's a man," Margaret interrupted. "A man who's just as down and out and trod on as you two have likely been. And if you took the time to look, I'd venture that you'd find a lot of the Hadley brothers in Handy Partree. In fact, I think you boys are starting to like him, no matter what you say. You can say you like fighting all you want, but I think that's what got you to throw those two fellows off Handy the other night."

"No, that can't be." Wilson had a confused frown about him now, not sure just what it was that Margaret was talking about. Why, it could be enough to befuddle him all over again; that it could. "We don't like . . . his type," he added, thinking twice before using the word "nigger" in her presence.

Margaret rose, gathering up their plates and now empty coffee cups. "You know, my Abel was about as hardheaded and opinionated as Will Carston," she said, speaking of her husband, who had been dead for the better part of six years now. "Some things he said were worthless. On the other hand, he said some things that made an awful lot of sense. For instance, he always claimed that any man who didn't change his mind about something over a ten-year period ought to be declared dead from the neck up. I think he was right." In silence she stacked the few dishes between her hands and was about to leave, when she added, "I never did consider you boys for being dead from the neck up. But maybe I was wrong."

Then she was gone. On her way to the kitchen, she muttered to Ella Mae, who had just come out of the kitchen with Rachel, "I want to talk to you before the evening's over."

At the same time Margaret disappeared into the kitchen, two of Marcus Easton's men—the one known as Walt, and a second one—entered Ferris House. Walt's nose was covered in some sort of makeshift bandage, likely from his earlier run-in with Dallas Bodeen in this same dining room. Neither one was looking any too happy as they scanned the interior of the dining area until they found what they were looking for—Ella Mae. The Hadleys didn't even notice them when they walked by, they were that caught up in their own thoughts. The two ruffians proceeded to the community table Ella Mae and Rachel had taken seats at.

"Come on, missy," Walt growled, grabbing Ella Mae by the arm and nearly dragging her away from the table. "Mr. Easton wants you."

"You let her go, you—" Rachel started to say before

being struck with Walt's hand hard across the face. The flat of his palm striking her face rang out like a shot, which got the Hadley brothers' attention.

"Don't even move," Walt's friend said, changing his point of aim from Ella Mae to the Hadleys. "Not unless you want to die fast."

"You wait till the Carstons get wind of this," Carny said, already trying to talk himself out of a bad situation. Anytime you had to deal with the business end of a loaded six-gun, it was a bad situation. But Walt's partner simply ignored him, although he was studying the faces of both of the brothers.

"Say Walt, don't these two look a lot like the ones that jumped us when we took after that nigger t'other night?" he said.

Walt, frowning, gave the Hadleys a quick glance and nodded in confirmation. "Yeah, now that you mention it."

"I say let's take them too," his partner said. "I got plans for these two."

Walt nodded again, a crooked grin coming to his face. "Might be fun after all."

"All right you two, let's have your guns." The Hadleys slowly took out their six-guns and placed them on the table before them. The gunman picked them up and stuck them in his waistband. Then, turning his gun on Rachel, who was still seated and on the verge of tears, he growled, "You too, young lady. You'll have to come too."

"Me?" Rachel was totally confused about what was taking place.

"Yeah, you."

"How come?" Walt asked his partner.

"Hey, you were the one who was dumb enough to waltz in here and announce that *Easton* was wanting her. Leave her behind, and she can identify us and the boss."

Any further conversation between the two stopped then and there, for it was at this point that Margaret Ferris entered the scene. "Just what the devil is going on out here?" she asked as she burst through the kitchen doors and made her way toward the group.

Walt had positioned Ella Mae between his gun, which was pointed at her belly, and Margaret, who was still coming toward them and didn't see his weapon.

"Mother!" Rachel cried in a weak yell.

"My God!" was all Margaret could say when she saw the tears in her daughter's eyes and the trickle of blood coming from the corner of her mouth. "Are you all right?" she asked as she quickened her pace across the room toward her daughter. "What have they—"

It was then Walt temporarily pulled Ella Mae to the side, stepped out in front of Margaret, and knocked her out with one harsh blow to the jaw.

CHAPTER

★ 23 ★

It was Handy Partree who discovered Margaret Ferris lying unconscious next to one of the community tables. Although his side still ached with a terrible throb, as it had all day, he had lost a good deal of sweat over the fire, as he'd done his damndest to complete all of the work Harvey Reed had lined up for him. But that didn't stop him from thinking of the joy he would have in visiting with Ella Mae again tonight. So, even with the pain he was experiencing, he had plowed through the work, hammering and hammering away, stopping only for a few minutes at the noon hour to eat a sandwich and some coffee Harvey Reed had personally gotten him from the Porter Cafe. He was sure it couldn't have been more than fifteen minutes from the time Harvey had handed him the food to the time he'd gone back to swinging that hammer. But then, as he had observed to Chance, Harvey Reed was a businessman above all else.

"Lordy," he had muttered as he entered Ferris House, saw Margaret lying there motionless, and rushed to her side, kneeling over her. She was out cold, that much he was sure of as he looked about for something to revive her with. The somewhat hot pot of coffee on the table wouldn't do a lick of good, so he rushed to the kitchen, slamming the door back against the wall as he entered. He stopped looking when he spotted a pitcher of what looked like cool water. Without hesitation he grabbed it and tore out of the room, kneeling down beside Margaret again, although a bit uncertain as to what to do next. She had a reddish lump on the side of her jaw, likely where she had gotten hit. He dug part of his fist into the pitcher, got three fingers wet and started patting the lump on her jaw, hoping he was doing the right thing. The only thing running through his mind at the moment was how good he was at carpentry and blacksmithing, and how much he didn't know about bronc busting and doctoring. That little grain of knowledge worried him something fierce.

"Jesus, Mary, and Joseph!" Dallas said as he entered the boardinghouse and saw Handy kneeling over Margaret Ferris. "What the hell—"

"Da's how I found her, Mr. Bodeen, I swear!" Handy said, more out of habit than anything else. Too often when a black man was found at the scene of something that smacked of violence, the first thing that happened was he was blamed for it, no matter what it was.

"I know you did, Handy, I know," Dallas said, patting Handy on the shoulder as he kneeled down beside Margaret on her other side. "That's a nasty-looking bruise she's got."

"Da's a fac'." Handy kept sticking his fingers inside the pitcher and patting Margaret's jawline.

"Anyone else around?" Dallas said, giving the room a quick glance and seeing absolutely no one.

"No." Abruptly, Handy stopped what he was doing, his line of thought shifting to his original reason for coming here—to see Ella Mae. Only she wasn't anywhere in sight. In one sudden motion he was on his feet, reaching down to the bottom of his stomach as his deep voice yelled, "Ella! Ella Mae?!"

"Rachel?"

But the whole place seemed to be missing guests or customers. It was as though everyone had either checked out or was conspicuously absent.

"I wonder where the hell they are?" Dallas asked, puzzled.

"Don' know," was all Handy could think to say. On the other hand, he had figured out what needed to be done next. "You all got a doctor man in dis town?" He worked his hands under Margaret Ferris and stood up, holding her as though she were a feather.

Dallas was pushing seventy from the north side, but it didn't take long to pick up on what Handy had in mind. Leading him to the door, he opened it for him and stepped outside on the boardwalk. Pointing halfway down the main street, he said, "Across the street and just a couple doors down from the saloon. I'll be over there directly. Will's gonna want to know about this."

Each man left in his respective direction, Dallas stopping twice on the way to the lawman's office to ask citizens he knew if they had seen Rachel or Ella Mae in the past few minutes. No one had, and by the time he got to Will Carston, he was a worried man.

"Come on, Will, trouble's a-brewing!" was all he had to say as he poked his head in the marshal's office. Will Carston, who had been looking at some wanted posters, tossed them down and planted his hat firmly on his head on the way out, Dallas giving him a quick run-through of events as he knew them while they made their way to Adam Riley's office.

Handy was standing by in the doctor's office, looking as helpless as he no doubt felt at the moment. "Doctor say—" he started to say, but by then Will Carston had shot through the door to the physician's patients' room, Dallas Bodeen on his way behind him.

"Get out of here, Will," Adam Riley said in a perturbed manner. "Can't you see I'm working on a patient?"

"I can see you got Margaret there," was all Will said, in a hard tone indicating he wasn't used to having his authority questioned. "Now, what the hell's going on?"

"Someone hit her mighty hard, likely with a fist," the doctor said. "If he'd laid the barrel of a pistol aside her jaw, it would likely be shattered. As it is, I don't think the jaw is broken. But it sure is going to be sore for a while. The thing now is to bring her to. I think she hit that floor awfully hard, and hit herself on the head when she did."

"Miss Ella Mae and Miss Rachel weren' nowheres around," Handy said, his size filling the doorway. His voice seemed flat as could be, as though he were doing little less than stating simple facts.

"That's right, Will," Dallas said in confirmation. "Like I said, they ain't no place to be found."

Will's face screwed up in a question mark. "Think someone kidnapped 'em?" he asked cautiously.

Dallas tossed an eyebrow up, cocking his head at the marshal. "Now that you mention it, I seen her talking to those Hadley brothers, the older ones, when I left Ferris House not an hour before."

Will didn't need but a split second to decide what their next action should be. He looked at Dallas and said, "I'm gonna stay here and see that old Adam does his job and brings Margaret to, right proper. Maybe she can help us piece this thing together."

Dallas nodded eagerly. "Right, Will."

"You get back over to the jail and tell Joshua I want him to head out to Chance's and tell him what's happened. Much as that boy brags about being single, I know he thinks the world of Rachel Ferris."

"Sure enough, Will." Dallas was getting excited enough to remind you of a hunting dog about to set out after a wily fox that's been raiding the chicken coop.

"Hold on a second, Dallas," Will added, and turned his attention to Handy. "Can you shoot, young man?" he asked in a stern tone.

"Damn straight," Handy said, which was all Will needed to know.

"Then you and Dallas will saddle up and ride out to the Hadley spread. It's time we paid them a social call, if you know what I mean," Will said. "The both of you can consider yourselves deputy marshals. Now git."

After Dallas rode to the jail to tell Will's deputy what the marshal had said, the two men rode their horses hard. They pulled their reins in to bring their horses to a halt in front of the Hadley house. Both

Handy and Dallas had a rifle at the ready as they came to a stop, ready for a fight.

"Ike, I need to see Wilson and Carny," Dallas said when the middle brother of the Hadley clan stepped out of the door. "Need to know where they been this afternoon and tonight."

Ike shrugged. "Wish I knew. I ain't seen 'em since this afternoon. Couldn't tell you where they are at all."

"Now, you wouldn't be stretching the blanket on me, would you, Ike?" Dallas asked in a serious tone.

"Believe me, Mr. Bodeen, when I see them, I'll send 'em in to see you folks, but I swear to you here and now that I ain't seen neither one of 'em for some time," Ike said, suddenly worried about what might be going on with his older brothers and the community of Twin Rifles.

"Dey got anything to do wit taking Ella Mae or Miss Rachel, dey likely dead men afore long," Handy growled.

"I'll remember that next time I see 'em," Ike Hadley said. And as Dallas and Handy rode away, they could see the man had a worried look about him.

Chance hurried up the stairs to Adam Riley's office, pushed the door open and saw Will standing there patiently. "What's going on, Pa?" he asked.

Before Will could answer, Dallas and Handy made their way into the doctor's office. "Neither one of those Hadleys is anywhere to be seen, Will," Dallas said. "Ike says he ain't seen 'em either."

Adam Riley stuck his head out of his patients' room and said, "She's coming to, Will. Asking for you, she is."

Will barged past the doctor and was soon at Margaret Ferris's side. "You just take it easy, darling, everything's gonna be all right," he was saying, picking up her hand and holding it gently in his own.

"They took them," she said weakly. "Ella Mae and Rachel, they took them."

"I know, Margaret, I've got Dallas and Handy out a-looking for the Hadleys now," Will said. "Won't be long afore we got 'em, you'll see."

Distress came to her eyes as she grabbed Will's hand and looked him straight in the eye. "No, Will, it wasn't the Hadleys at all. They took Ella Mae and Rachel and Wilson and Carny Hadley. They took all four of 'em."

"Will someone tell me what in the hell is going on?" Chance asked in a mean and worried voice.

It was at this point that Will, Dallas, and Handy explained what each of them knew.

CHAPTER
★ **24** ★

They found Abe Forrest alone in Ernie Johnson's saloon. It was just as well, for if they had found any of his cohorts within sight, they would have killed them on the spot. It was turning into one of those nights.

"How about a beer, Chance?" Ernie asked the older Carston as he pushed open the bat-wing doors to Johnson's saloon, a meaner than hell look about him. The bartender/proprietor knew Chance was on the warpath, and offering him a beer seemed about the best way—if not the easiest—to calm him down. Hell, Chance hardly ever refused a brew.

"Not now, Ernie," Chance growled. As he spoke he glanced around the saloon. The usual evening crowd was there, but none of David Workman's crew could be seen. Except for Marshal Abe Forrest, who had a table all to himself.

Handy was with Chance and looked just as mean, so no one even made a suggestion that he leave Ernie Johnson's, whether they liked the color of his skin or not.

"Evening, Carston," Forrest said as Chance approached his table. "Have a seat and I'll buy you a beer." He was starting to stand up as he spoke, which was when Chance lashed out at him with a huge fist and hit him in the mouth, knocking him ass over teakettle as he fell backward out of his chair.

Ernie Johnson was going to say something, for he didn't allow fighting in his establishment, but Chance Carston had the floor and didn't seem in the mood to be interrupted, so Ernie wisely kept his mouth shut.

"What did you do with them, you sorry son of a bitch?" Chance said in a deadly voice. By the time he was finished speaking, he had his Colt's Conversion Model .44 in his hand, the long barrel pointed right at Abe Forrest's bread basket.

"What?" the marshal asked in bewilderment as he rubbed his jaw. "What the hell are you talking about? Who is 'them'?"

"The safest place for you right now is on that floor, mister, cause if you git up, I'm gonna hit you again." Mad didn't come anywhere close to describing what Chance Carston was feeling right then.

"And eff he don', I will," Handy said with a frown and an equal amount of frustration.

"Ella Mae and Rachel Ferris is who I'm talking about."

Abe Forrest's eyebrows were suddenly knit together in a frown of their own, for he obviously didn't know the women Chance had just named. "I have no idea what you're talking about, Carston," he said, and made his way to his feet. "As for hitting me, let's go see your local law. There must be something on the books in this two-bit town about assaulting a lawman."

A snarl curled up on Chance's lip. "Suits me fine. I'll show you the way."

In Will Carston's office a vehement Abe Forrest vented his rage and demanded an arrest. "I want to know what you're going to do about it!" the lawman from Panhandle demanded, striking one fist into the palm of the other hand.

"And what have you got to say for yourself?" Will said when he turned to his son. Chance was always getting into trouble of one sort or another, just barely managing to get out of it as often as not. In fact, Will often found himself wondering that the boy had lived as long as he had.

As mad as he was, Chance found it in him to plant a grin on his face. "Nothing except he claims you run a two-bit town," he said, knowing full well it would ruffle his father's feathers.

"That a fact, is it?" Will said, cocking a frowning eye toward Abe Forrest. "Two-bit town, is it?" He took an aggressive step toward the marshal from Panhandle and poked a stubby finger in the man's chest, the force of it pushing him back a bit. "Well, let me tell you something, mister. In this *two-bit town,* as you call it, I don't stand for no fighting, so Chance was wrong in the way he went at approaching you. On the other hand, that's pretty much how my son is, direct approach and all. But one other thing I won't stand for in Twin Rifles is kidnapping, and more important than your piddle-ass fight is the fact that two women in our town are missing. I don't suppose you'd know anything about that, would you?"

Frustrated, Abe Forrest had apparently had it with

dealing with the people in Twin Rifles. "I don't know what it is with you folks about being repetitious, but like I already told your son——"

Will Carston was fed up with the way things were going too. With two quick hands he grabbed Forrest by the shirt front and pulled him close, the look on his own face deadly. "I don't care what you told Chance, I'm the one who's asking you now, so don't give me no smart-alecky talk or I'm liable to toss you in the hoosegow just for looking mean," he said through gritted teeth. "Now, answer my question, mister. Answer it!" With this last he shook the man before him, as though the extra motion would spur his memory.

It did the trick, for Abe Forrest suddenly had a look filled with both concern and fear, if that were possible. Chance also thought he saw a bit of revelation in those eyes.

"Look, it's like I said, I don't know who these women are or what's happened to them," he said, somewhat regaining his composure. "But if someone's taken them, I'd say I wouldn't put it past David Workman and his bunch." His eyes fell on Handy, who had silently stood off to the side as he'd entered the lawman's office, knowing that Will and Chance Carston could handle what needed taking care of just fine. "You and your friends have made Workman and his crew awful disappointed, Handy. He's wanting you for that Gentry killing so bad he can taste it." Then, facing Will again, he nodded and said, "Yeah, if you're lacking for suspects, Marshal, I'd take a prime look at David Workman. What you're describing sounds like something low-down enough that he'd be a part of it."

"Where Workman be?" Handy said. No beating

around the bush. Like Chance, it wasn't Handy's way.

Forrest shrugged. "When I left him, he was camped outside of town by a creek." He paused a moment before adding, "Look, if there's anything I can do to help . . . I mean, if Workman is involved in this scheme . . . well, I want you to know I don't approve of it and had nothing to do with it. Nothing at all."

But his words fell on deaf ears as Chance pulled out his six-gun and began checking the loads, readying for battle. "Workman strikes me as being too goddamn dumb to try and find a hideout of some sort."

"He full of hisself all right," Handy said with a nod.

"Bullheaded enough to snatch those girls up and hold 'em until we come for 'em," Will said in agreement. "But don't you go planning on nothing for tonight, Chance."

"But—"

"Look, you start shooting in the dark, and one of us or one of them is likely to hit one of those girls, and that's the last thing I want, son," Will said in a firm tone.

Chance holstered his Colt. "I see what you mean. What, then, hit 'em at dawn?"

A wily grin came over Will Carston. "Worked fine for them Comancheros, as I recall." It had been several years since Will had discovered his wife, Cora, killed by Comancheros. He would never forget the sight of her, lying there dead. Nor would he forget the way he and his sons had tracked down the Comancheros and broke into their camp at daybreak, guns blazing, killing the lot of them without mercy.

"Yeah." Chance's grin was just as wily and full of memory as his father's.

"Where you going?" Will asked when Handy headed for the door.

"Dey's things still need taking care of," was all he'd say as his big frame left Will's office.

Will would have asked him just what he was talking about, but there was a certain excitement in his own thoughts that dismissed Handy's actions for now. There was plenty of time to discuss it later.

CHAPTER
★ 25 ★

Fine mess you got us into," Wilson growled to Carny that night as the sun set. Both had been taken to the creek area where David Workman had made camp, the same area the Hadleys had had their talk with Workman only the day before. With them, of course, had come the two women, Ella Mae and Rachel. The women seemed awfully scared, Wilson noted on the way to the creek, and with good reason. It didn't take a genius to figure out that they had been taken with a dual purpose in mind, both of which concerned the Negro woman, Ella Mae.

First off, plain and simple, this Easton character was taking her back to wherever he came from, with Ella Mae in tow. He didn't seem to care one way or the other what she may have thought about the idea, he was flat out taking her back. But then, that was how

The Stranger from Nowhere

those plantation managers were, a hard, stubborn breed if ever there was one.

The second reason for having Ella Mae in camp was to draw Handy Partree out to the creek. Putting the girl in some sort of danger was Workman's way of forcing Partree's hand. Still, it didn't seem to matter a lick, considering the two of them were now tied together next to a tree by the creek.

"Oh, shut up, Wilson," Carny said back to his brother, "you ain't got nothing to brag about."

"Both of you shut up!" one of the guards said to them, and they had both shut their mouths.

When dark had come, both of the Hadleys had engaged in bits of sleep here and there as they tried to figure out how they would get out of this fix. What they knew for sure was that Rachel would likely get killed for witnessing what she had, and that they would likely meet the same fate.

"There's gotta be a way," Wilson softly growled to himself around midnight as he stirred about. It surprised him that Carny wasn't about to argue the point with him. What he heard next was what really startled him.

"Hush now," he recognized Handy Partree saying in a low voice. He cut loose their bonds. "You sit still like nothin' happened," he added. Then he quietly stuck a six-gun in each of their fists. "You be ready to fight come daylight."

Then he was gone into the night.

What the hell was Handy Partree doing helping them out? It was a mystery, pure and simple.

The sun hadn't been up half an hour when the Carstons boldly rode into David Workman's camp. Will, Chance, and Wash all dismounted, leaving their

201

horses ground-tied, making sure their guns were ready in their holsters as they looked for Workman.

"Kind of early, ain't it, lawman?" Workman said in a cranky mood.

"You wouldn't know the whereabouts of two women, now, would you, Workman?" Will asked in as official a tone as he could muster. "Young black girl named Ella Mae and a white woman named Rachel Ferris?"

"No, I damn sure wouldn't. What's it to you?" If being ornery was what this man specialized in, he was very good at showing it.

"You'd better produce 'em and be quick about it," Chance said in an all-business tone. "You've got about one minute before I start taking you and your camp apart piece by piece."

David Workman gave out a loud guffaw; a crude sort of laugh, Chance thought.

"Best listen to him, Workman," Handy's own loud voice said off to the side of camp. In fact, he was speaking from the vicinity of the tree where Wilson and Carny Hadley had been tied up the night before. But now they weren't tied up. They had been freed of their bonds and held six-guns in their hands, ready to use the revolvers when called upon. "You ain' got no chance."

By now the rest of Workman's crew were up and armed, ready for a fight if their boss called for it. "Sullivan!" Workman called out, and one of his men stood up, hauling each of the women to their feet, Ella Mae and Rachel Ferris. But rather than use them for a shield, he was foolish enough to stand one on each side of him, which was a dreadful mistake.

Handy Partree brought his rifle up to his shoulder,

took dead aim on the man's chest, and fired once. Sullivan dropped to the ground, dead.

It was all that was needed to open the ball. Workman went for his gun but wasn't fast enough. Chance pulled his Colt from his holster and shot him twice in the chest, knowing he was dead by the time he fell to the ground.

Handy ran toward the women, intent on bringing them to the ground and out of harm's way. But he took two slugs on the way to save them, and when he fell on them, he was bleeding, although he was sure they were safe and out of harm's reach now.

Will and Wash drew their own six-guns and fired point-blank at a handful of Workman's crew, killing them where they stood as they tried to make a fight of it.

Wilson and Carny Hadley both opened up on the two men who had shot Handy, killing them on sight as well. Neither one of the Hadleys, however, was hit. In fact, with the exception of Handy, all of the rescuers were standing tall.

"You all right, Handy?" Wilson said as he rushed to the big man's side. Partree had taken a shot high in the chest and in his arm, and was doing a good deal of bleeding. Without waiting for an answer, Wilson untied his neckerchief and retied it around Handy's arm, momentarily stopping the bleeding, he thought.

"It's going to be fine," Ella Mae said in a voice that didn't seem to be scared at all. "Yes, everything is going to be fine," she said again, and Wilson noticed that she was hugging Handy something fierce.

But then, that was exactly what Miss Rachel was doing to Chance Carston too.

CHAPTER
★ 26 ★

Not everyone died that day at David Workman's camp on the creek. The guard who came to check on the Hadley brothers and wound up being subdued by Handy Partree just as the Carstons rode into camp was very much alive. Also alive was one of the men who had taken part in the shootout but, having been wounded, had the good sense to stay on the ground once he had been shot. As hot and heavy as the bullets had been flying that morning, he likely would have died on the spot had he tried to fight it out like some of his companions. Both of these men, when questioned by Will Carston, admitted that it was David Workman's idea to kidnap Ella Mae and use her to try to draw Handy into the Workman camp.

"I don't know why they took the other woman," one of them said in puzzlement.

"Whatever brought it about, it was one hell of a mistake, I can tell you that," Chance said with a frown and a snarl as he watched his father interrogate the men.

"Had something to do with those two men who were riding with that Easton fella," the other commented. "The plantation owner who was wanting the Negro girl back for his own."

"Like I said, it was a hell of a mistake."

The women hadn't been harmed. Mostly, they had been scared to death. And when Wilson Hadley had rushed over and checked on the fallen Handy, Carny had grabbed up the guard's bowie knife, cut the women free of their bonds and pulled off their gags. That was when Ella Mae had taken Handy in her arms and said everything was going to be all right. It was also when Rachel had rushed to Chance's side, throwing her arms about him as though she hadn't seen him in a year and he had just returned from battle unscathed.

"That girl's right," Chance had whispered to Rachel while she held him, "it's gonna be all right." Rachel had stayed right at Chance's side as he watched Will question what was left of David Workman's crew.

Wash had taken to doctoring up Handy as best he could, while the Hadleys had liberated the firearms of the dead bodies strewn throughout camp. They didn't seem to feel guilty about the prospect of stripping a bunch of dead men. Were they able to do it themselves, they would have taken every last one of those rifles and six-guns into Kelly's Hardware in town and sell them for a goodly profit. But even the Hadleys knew the rule that Marshal Will Carston had set in motion concerning these types of shootings. All weapons would be collected and kept in the possession of

205

the marshal, who would sell them to Kelly's Hardware on occasion when the city coffers were low on funds and needing a bit of extra cash.

"I didn't see that Easton character around anywhere, Pa, did you?" Chance asked when Will was done with his questions.

"Come to think of it, no."

"We're gonna have to get Handy into Doc Riley's soon as we can," Wash interrupted, a hint of concern in his voice. "I don't know how good that bandaging of mine is going to do. This is more Sarah Ann's department."

Ever the organizer and man-in-charge, Will Carston took the reins now. "All right, here's what we'll do. Wash, you and Chance take Handy and the girls back to town. The Hadleys will give me a hand with these carcasses and straightening the camp up. Wouldn't want to pollute the water or nothing."

The Carston brothers did as they were told, gathering up the mounts for Handy, Rachel, and Ella Mae. But just before they left camp, Chance took in a sight he never thought he'd see in his own lifetime. Will Carston had approached the Hadleys and was sticking his hand out in friendship.

"By the way, boys, I want to tell you how grateful I am for having you and Handy on our side this morning," he said in a sincere tone. "Without your help, I reckon we'd have taken in more lead than we did."

Wilson and Carny both shook Will's hand, a look of disbelief about them as they did. Finally they looked at one another, and Wilson said, "I reckon she was right."

Carny could only nod in affirmation. "Yeah."

"What's that?" Will asked.

"Nothing, Marshal, nothing," Wilson said, as though to dismiss his words.

Will shrugged. "If you say so," he said; and went about trying to straighten up the camp.

The Hadley brothers, on the other hand, would never dismiss what they were thinking. For what was crossing both of their minds was what Margaret Ferris had said about helping someone out when they really needed it, and the way those people would react toward them. By God, she had been right!

The only thing on Chance's mind as they rode back to Twin Rifles—other than the thought that Rachel was safe at his side—was the fact that he hadn't seen Marcus Easton anywhere near the Workman camp. This led him to wonder exactly where this scoundrel could be found, for if he had anything to do with David Workman, Chance was sure the man was a devilish rascal, at the very least. He decided it was worth keeping an eye out for him, especially since he was nowhere to be found.

They galloped down the main street, which was just starting to show some life as the sun came into full view on the horizon, and pulled up in front of Adam Riley's office.

"Got a customer for you, Doc," Chance said as he helped a silent Handy Partree into the physician's office.

"Now I can understand why Will keeps asking you what kind of trouble you're in this time," Adam said with a knowing grin. "Every time I see you, either you or the man with you is bleeding like a sieve."

"At least you ain't sitting around twiddling your thumbs, Doc," Chance said in half seriousness.

"True, but I don't think I need a major surgery case

every time you walk into my office." Adam helped Handy lie down, and prepared to take off his shirt and work on him.

Ella Mae was soon at his side, Handy's big hand encased in both of hers, a worried smile on her face as she said, "The doctor will take care of you fine, Handy. I'll be back to see you later in the day and we'll talk about that English of yours."

He gave her a weak smile, squeezed her hands and said, "Yes, ma'am, Miss Ella Mae."

Then she was gone, before he could see the tears begin to flow down her cheeks.

A look of shock came to Rachel's face, as though a stark realization had just come to mind, which it had. "Oh my God, who's running Ferris House?"

Adam Riley glanced over his shoulder and smiled. "I suspect your mother is, Rachel. I think she's a lot tougher than most of us give her credit for."

"But the marshal said—"

"Yes, she got knocked down and knocked out," he continued. "I patched her up and told her to take it easy for a couple of days, but when I stopped by your establishment this morning to check on her, there she was, holding down the fort all by herself. A remarkable woman, I'll say that much."

"I'd better get over there and help her," Rachel said as she made a hasty run for the door, obviously on her way to Ferris House.

Chance headed for the door too, stopped, turned to face Adam Riley. But the doctor instinctively knew what he was about to say.

"I know, Chance, put it on your bill," he said, and went back to working on Handy Partree.

* * *

Chance wasn't far behind Rachel when she entered Ferris House. He'd given up a good breakfast meal to meet the Workman crew this morning, and his stomach was now telling him it was time to make up for the meal he had missed. Luckily, the morning crowd was thinning out, with only a handful of customers still eating. He took a seat at the end of the community table nearest the entrance, where Dallas Bodeen was sopping up what was left on his plate.

"I take it you and your pa and brother were successful at getting the young ladies back," Dallas said with a smile.

"You could say that."

"Seen both of 'em come flying in here like a house afire. Headed for the kitchen to check on Miss Margaret, I reckon."

As much as he wanted to share Dallas's good feelings, a frown formed on Chance's forehead. "I wouldn't get to feeling too easy about it yet, Dallas. I got a notion this shindig ain't quite over." He then went on to briefly describe their encounter with Workman, putting particular emphasis on the fact that Marcus Easton was nowhere to be found, although the surviving outlaws claimed he was a part of the plot to kidnap the women. By the time he was through talking, Dallas had lost his joyous look.

"Reckon I'll have to keep an eye out for those fellers." Dallas drained his coffee cup, plunked on his hat and left. If another word needed to be spoken, Chance didn't know what it was.

"Sorry to be so late getting to you, Chance." He looked up, and there was Margaret Ferris, poised to take his order. She had what Chance had once heard

209

Doc Riley refer to as a compress—whatever the hell that was—on the side of her jaw, covering the bruise she likely had there, but other than that, she seemed little the worse for wear. Adam Riley was right, this was really a wondrous woman. "What can I do for you?"

Chance gave her a gentle smile, hoping she would take it the right way. "Feeling better, are you, Margaret?"

Her smile was one of relief. "Yes, especially now that I've got my daughter and my maid back." She came around the end of the table, leaned over and kissed him in a kindhearted way. "Thanks, Chance. You don't know how much I appreciate it."

He told her he was hungry enough to eat whatever she had on the Dutch oven in her kitchen, and she smiled at him again and wrote something down on her order pad.

"By the way, Margaret," he said as she prepared to head for the kitchen, "you were right about the Hadleys. Came in real handy when Workman and his crew got uppity."

"I told you they didn't have anything to do with taking the girls, didn't I?"

"Yes, ma'am, you did." It was about as close as either of them would ever hear Chance Carston come to being apologetic, and both knew it.

A few minutes later, when Margaret was serving Chance coffee, the doors burst open and Marcus Easton came barging into Ferris House, followed by his two men. He looked as mean as hell, and in his own mind he had a right to be. He was even carrying a whip in one hand. Knowing the man was a plantation owner or manager of some sort, Chance had a good idea what it was he had in mind this visit.

"Get that bitch out here, lady!" he ordered, suddenly acting as though he were in command of the place.

As much as she had been through, Margaret Ferris seemed unflappable. "You mean Ella Mae," she corrected him. She knew just as well as Chance what the man's intentions were and who it was he wanted. If this bully had made any such reference to Rachel, using the language he just did on Ella Mae, Margaret would have scratched his eyes out by now.

"Watch your mouth, mister," Chance said. "That's a lady you're talking to."

"You mind your own business," the one called Walt said in a smart-alecky way. Apparently, he thought he was king of the hill too, for he only said it once.

"Come on, get her out here!" Easton demanded again.

There are times when a man does things by instinct, times when he relies on his gut feeling about something and follows that feeling no matter what. That was just what Chance had done when he'd taken his seat at the community table. Normally, he would sit closest to the kitchen, for he liked to see Rachel walk back and forth with her orders, liked taking in the shape of her, no matter what he told everyone else about him being a lifelong bachelor and all. But this morning he'd taken the seat next to Dallas, partly to let him know he should keep an eye open for Easton and his cronies. He had also done something unusual for him, laying his Stetson flat on the table before him, rather than placing it on a peg to his rear and against the wall. The hat and its brim were just big enough to conceal his Colt's Conversion Model, which suited him fine. So if any of these pilgrims wanted to dance, he didn't feel squeamish in the least about offering to open the ball.

211

Marcus Easton didn't have to wait long for what he wanted, for the next person to walk out of the kitchen was Ella Mae herself. But Chance could tell by the expression on her face, a determined look if ever he had seen one, that this woman hadn't come out to submit to whatever this man had in mind.

"Get over here, you cheap bitch!" he all but yelled at her.

But Ella Mae wasn't having any more of Marcus Easton's bossiness, not now and never again. From the fold of her apron she pulled out the Walker Colt that Margaret Ferris had used to scare this man only a few days ago. And that gun, as Chance recalled hearing it, was empty. He found himself wondering if this woman knew how many times you could run a bluff before it came back on you.

"No, Marcus Easton, I'm not going to tolerate you and your bully mouth anymore," she said, slowly raising the gun with both hands and aiming it directly at his chest.

"Put that damn thing down," he ordered her, "you're not going to shoot anyone, least of all me." As these words came out, a bit of a sneer came to his lips.

It was the wrong thing to do.

Feeling bold, Marcus Easton took a long stride toward Ella Mae, apparently intent on taking the gun from her hands. But he never did accomplish that, for in one motion she cocked the Walker Colt and fired it. The bullet hit him square in the chest, knocking him back off his feet as though a mountain had fallen on him. He fell to the floor in a lifeless pile of flesh and bones. The roar of the six-gun was deafening, to say the least, as its echo vibrated back and forth inside Ferris House. As she had fired it, Ella Mae had staggered backward, but then regained her balance.

The horror of what she had done was evident in her eyes.

Walt didn't turn out to be as brave as he had let on, and turned tail and ran out the front door as soon as Ella Mae's gun had gone off. His partner, on the other hand, decided to play out his hand right then and there and went for his gun. Chance brushed away his Stetson, grabbed his own Colt and shot the man before he could clear leather. He was sure the man was dead by the time he fell to the floor.

No sooner had Chance gotten to his feet to pursue Walt, than he heard a third shot, this one from out front of the house. Gun in hand, he rushed to the door, pulled it open and stepped outside on the boardwalk, expecting a fight of sorts. What he saw was Walt, six-gun in hand, slumped against a water trough, motionless. Standing there in the middle of the street, his Henry rifle smoking, was Dallas Bodeen.

"Loudmouth son of a bitch," Dallas growled as he took in the figure of the dead man.

Chance stepped a little closer, saw the man was indeed not among the living. "He ain't no more, hoss," was all he said. "He ain't no more."

CHAPTER
★ 27 ★

It was close to a week before Handy felt good enough to get up on his own and move about. He had done a lot of thinking during those days in bed, and gotten quite confused about the conclusions he had come to. He had been visited by Ella Mae, the Carston men, and the Ferris women, not to mention Harvey Reed, who continually reminded him that there was work piling up at the livery for him. But he hadn't seen the Hadley brothers, and it was they who he had wanted to talk to the most. Although he would never admit it to anyone, least of all them, he thought the three of them had made a pretty good team out there at Workman's camp. Still, they hadn't come to see him at all, and he could only interpret that as meaning that they still didn't like him. After all, they were the ones who had first insulted him when he'd ridden into Twin

Rifles. With that foremost in mind, he made his decision.

"Well, I'm glad to see you're up and around, Handy," a smiling Ella Mae said to him when he entered Ferris House. "But why look so sad?"

"I'm leaving," he said, and there was indeed a sadness in his voice, as though he didn't want to leave.

"But why?" Ella Mae asked, confused at his words.

Before she could get an answer, the door flew open and in marched Harvey Reed, followed by Will Carston. "There he is, Marshal! See, I told you he was leaving. Can't you talk some sense into him, Will?" Harvey Reed spoke in what could only be a pleading manner, indicative of a man who is desperate about something.

"Leaving, are you, Handy?" Will asked.

"Yeah, ain' much for me here," the big man said.

"Ain't much! What do you mean, ain't much!" Harvey all but yelled. He was a man about to pull his hair out, he was that excited over Handy's departure. "Why, I got a week and a half worth of work piled up at the livery. Ain't much, my eye and Betty Martin!"

"But Harvey, you said it yourself, ain' nuttin' but strangers makes trouble in you town," Handy said with a good deal of remorse, "and I ain' nuttin' but trouble. Ask anyone."

"Well, that's what I said, Handy," the livery man stuttered, "but that ain't quite what I meant."

"Oh?"

"Why sure. See, you ain't a stranger anymore. Why, you've met nearly half the town since you been here, and you just got to give the rest of 'em a chance to get to know you better."

Handy was still uncertain of himself, and said, "I don't know."

Suddenly, Harvey Reed's expression changed from one of desperation to one of total surprise. His eyes open wide, he said in awe, "You called me Harvey."

The whole thing seemed to have taken Handy by surprise too. "Yeah, I did." It was as though he couldn't believe what he had just said.

"Well, you gotta stay now, Handy," Harvey said. Then, in one last try, he turned to Will Carston. "Come on, Will, ain't there something you can say or do to make him stay?"

"Gee, I don't know, Harvey," was his reply as he pushed his hat back and scratched his head as though in thought. After a moment, he added, "Of course, there is the investigation and all."

"Investigation?" It didn't sound like a friendly word to Handy at all, and he found himself backing off from it.

"Why sure. I sent the Hadleys back to Panhandle with Abe Forrest, along with the bodies of Workman and his bunch, not to mention the waddies who survived it all. Told 'em ary I ever see 'em within a hundred miles of Twin Rifles, I'd shoot 'em and feed 'em to the buzzards. Got the point real quick, they did."

"That don' sound like a investigation." So that was why the Hadleys hadn't come to see him; they had been sent away on a mission. Handy felt his heart lift a great deal; in fact, he felt a whole lot better about not seeing them.

"By the way, Wilson and Carny said they wanted to see you when they git back," Will said. "First time I seen 'em act civil toward a man with the color of skin you got. Unbelievable, I tell you."

"But what 'bout this investigation?" Handy asked, still curious.

216

"Oh, that. Well, I convinced Forrest to do some more checking into that shooting up in Panhandle," Will explained. "Said I'd keep an eye on you while he did, for he'll be getting back to me in a month or two. I convinced him that Workman fella wasn't telling the whole truth, and he about believes me. So you want to leave or not, I reckon you'll have to let me know where you're a-going . . . and not go far at that."

"Looks like you're stuck here, whether you like it or not." Ella Mae smiled.

A slow smile came to Handy's face, and he reached out and took Ella Mae's hand in his. "Well, maybe 'tis for the bes'," he said. "Got a lot of hammerin' to do, and I das not disappoint Harvey Reed."

"Now you're talking, Handy." Harvey grinned, feeling much better as he slapped Handy on the back. "Now you're talking."

Back in the kitchen, Rachel was prattling on to Chance about how she had felt when Easton's men had kidnapped them, and how terrified she was about the whole event. It sometimes amazed Chance how the woman was able to do more than one thing at a time, like gab and prepare a meal all at once. It had been a week now since the shooting and kidnapping, and she couldn't get over talking about it. Or was that her excuse for having him nearby? He found himself wondering if she missed him as much as he had missed her, even for that short period of time. Finally he stood back, set down his cup of coffee and chuckled.

"That's the trouble with you women," he said, still grinning down at her.

Rachel looked up at him, raising a curious eyebrow. "And what, pray tell, is that?"

"You talk too much."

Going back to her work, acting as though she were ignoring him, Rachel said, "Mother says it's a woman's right to talk as much as she—"

Chance took her by the shoulders as she spoke and turned her to him. "I don't give a damn what your mother says."

Then he leaned down and kissed her warm and hard.

She didn't seem to care what her mother said either, then.

Not one bit.

Printed in the United States
By Bookmasters